ALSO BY JON PINEDA

FICTION

Apology

NONFICTION

Sleep in Me

POETRY

Little Anodynes
The Translator's Diary
Birthmark

LET'S NO ONE GET HURT

Let's No One Get Hurt

JON PINEDA

FARRAR, STRAUS AND GIROUX | NEW YORK

Farrar, Straus and Giroux
175 Varick Street, New York 10014

Grateful acknowledgment is made to the editors at Persea Books for
permission to reprint the following previously published material:
excerpt from "A Scavenger's Ode to the Turntable" by Patrick Rosal,
from *Brooklyn Antediluvian*. Copyright © 2016 by Patrick Rosal.
Reprinted with the permission of Persea Books, Inc. (New York),
www.perseabooks.com. All rights reserved.

Library of Congress Cataloging-in-Publication Data
Names: Pineda, Jon, 1971– author.
Title: Let's no one get hurt / Jon Pineda.
Description: First edition. | New York : Farrar, Straus and Giroux, 2018.
Identifiers: LCCN 2017038289 | ISBN 9780374185244 (hardcover)
Subjects: LCSH: Teenage girls—Fiction. | Rich people—Fiction. |
    GSAFD: Bildungsromans.
Classification: LCC PS3616.I565 L48 2018 | DDC 813/.6—dc23
LC record available at https://lccn.loc.gov/2017038289

Designed by Richard Oriolo

Our books may be purchased in bulk for promotional, educational, or
business use. Please contact your local bookseller or the Macmillan
Corporate and Premium Sales Department at 1-800-221-7945, extension
5442, or by e-mail at MacmillanSpecialMarkets@macmillan.com.

www.fsgbooks.com
www.twitter.com/fsgbooks • www.facebook.com/fsgbooks

1   3   5   7   9   10   8   6   4   2

for Kundiman

. . . we were learning to turn anything into anything else

—Patrick Rosal, "A Scavenger's Ode to the Turntable"

LET'S NO ONE GET HURT

IF I CONCENTRATE, I CAN see where the river should be. It almost doesn't exist, like the blue of skim milk. Or tailor's chalk I've watched Dox brush away after sealing a stitch. But I know it's there. The river waits for me, and that's all that matters.

My father shuts off the engine. The pickup rattles. We sit and stew. After a bit, we can smell the random field. It's been torn open, that's what I say. My father winces. In my head, he corrects me: "Aspire to precision, Pearl." When he talks this way, I feel like he's gone back in time, like I'm one of his students being forced to listen to him.

"Pearl," my father says now but doesn't say anything else. It means get out. It means, at the very least, get a handle on the dog. Marianne Moore is off the pickup and jumps the grass ditch. Though the dog has bad hips, she is doing smooth ovals, making a dirt necklace in the open field. She is smiling.

I slam the truck door. There's a tinny ring, even though the sides are mostly rust and primer. I grab a shovel and some rope from the back. There are mouth-sized holes in the truck bed. Marianne Moore hunkers down like she's already been shot.

MY EYES FOLLOW WHERE THE rows of broken earth head north. They end on the spongy loam. From there mix gaps of pale sky and lit leaf canopies the amber of fresh motor oil. The river is just on the other side of those trees. It's a smear of acrylic. On the river's surface float plywood skiffs and other vessels of scrap wood.

For the last few years I've had no choice but to become someone else. I've been around these kinds of boats, these quick creations. Sterns weighed down with piecemeal outboard motors, the shells endlessly dented out of frustration. Metal casings entirely removed. The dampened guts of tinkered-with chokes puff, held open by paint-coated screwdrivers and pastel pink putty.

Everything is makeshift.

My father reaches behind the bench seat, unzips one end of the leather case I'd sewn for him myself, Dox having been good enough to show me how on a scavenged sewing machine. My father pulls out the shotgun like he's unsheathing a sword. He breaks the gun's neck and checks the empty barrels out of habit.

He picks up a crushed box from the floorboard and shakes

it, then slips into his suit-vest pocket the last of the shells, lip-stick red and the size of quartered candlesticks. His vest is a light blue pinstripe. It's a miniature of the tilled field, a riffle where the river shallows.

My father has become the kind of man who likes to wear a vest without a shirt. He is ripe and smells like what I remember of store-bought spices, back when my mother used to do all the shopping. He's a dank mixture of cumin and turmeric, if I'm trying. His graying hair reaches past his shoulders. I turn my head the moment I see his nipples peek out from the sides of the vest. His nipples are brown and wrinkled like pecan meat.

"You ready?" he says.

"I think so."

"Either you are or you aren't."

"Okay."

"Precision, Pearl."

"I'm *prepared* to do this one thing that will make you proud of me."

"That's better. That's my girl."

"How come we have to do this?"

"Because she should've been put down a long time ago."

I let that sit out there for a bit.

"Pearl?"

I try to nod.

I hate when he calls me his girl. Not because I can't be anyone's girl, but because if I'm anyone's girl, I'd have to be his by default. I'm trying to make peace with this idea. It's been getting more difficult. The more I catch glimpses of what kind of man he really is.

Marianne Moore curls up the size of an alligator snapper, or one of those antique circular hatboxes I've found in one of the hallway closets of the boathouse. She waits for us in the dirt. I could kick her where she is and send her rolling between the rows. Sometimes I want nothing more than to let her have it. Don't get me wrong, I love her, but I can't help thinking about how that would look, the dog on her back like a flipped turtle, with her legs going through the motions all herky-jerky.

My father and I walk the field. I carry the shovel. There's a skin of rust on the shovel's head. It's been put to the test a time or two. My father cradles the shotgun in the crook of his arm. In these moments, it's as if he's bought into this new life—*hook, line, and sinker.*

In the air of the open field there's the tang of gun oil my father wiped over both barrels. I hold the shovel in one hand and the splintered rope in the other. If I squint like my father, the rope is a single line that leads to Marianne Moore's neck.

"Princess," I say, and the dog smiles back, I swear. Like sweet Dox, she has lost most of her teeth. My father calls it a survivor's smile. Whatever it is, it's painful to take note of.

"This is for her own good," my father says.

I know it, though I don't let on.

He wants me to put the dog out of her misery, but instead, I'm going to turn her body into lace.

MY FATHER WON'T TALK ABOUT who we used to be because that would mean talking about her, my mother, and what she did to the both of us. I don't happen to think it was so bad, but that's just me.

"You're as crazy as her," my father would say if he could read my mind.

I picture my father and me someday striking out for an unknown future. This time the pickup loaded down with every item from the boathouse we share with the two men.

"No Dox and no Fritter," he says.

"We'll just leave them?"

"Damn straight."

I laugh. "They took us in, and we'll just leave them."

"They didn't take us in."

"What do you call it then?"

"They scooted over."

"They did more than that."

"Fine. They made room."

"Piss-poor explanation."

He's the one who laughs now.

"Well, they deserve more," I say.

"We all deserve more."

"They're grown men who've worked hard, and now—"

My father does a spit take. The air burns, and he shakes his head. "That's a generous assessment. You're always so generous, Pearl."

I decide not to bite.

"You know what they say about you?" I try my best not to make a face.

"One can only imagine."

"They say you're the best friend anyone could ask for."

"You lie."

"Dox does, at least."

"Dox is a good egg."

"And Fritter?"

My father can only show me his teeth. They're chipped mostly, the middle two flat as sugar cubes.

"What?" I say.

"You tell me."

Fritter, at over three hundred pounds, resembles multiple copies of Dox sewn together. Unlike Dox, Fritter is motor-oil black, like he was spit out of some great big flame-shooting engine. His dreadlocks are a spectrum of burnt orange. When they're not swept back, they writhe. It's a wonder the two are even related.

When I used to think there was a future for me, I imagined myself becoming a translator, like my mother had wanted to be. The last time I offered the idea up, it was over a dinner of crayfish we'd trapped ourselves and chanterelles Dox scooped from the surrounding woods. My father said it was a nice thought and hoped the world would stick around long enough for it to happen.

"Where's it going?" I'd asked.

I don't know why I even bothered.

"The world?" my father said.

"Yeah."

"Probably to sleep."

Dox, glowing at a distance, shook his head. He started the opening riff of "Drown" by Son Volt. The song had the misfortune of having been left on a mixtape in the pickup. I could relate.

My father's cough pulled me back.

"Best we can hope for, Pearl, is that it'll just close its eyes and never wake up."

Dox worked the slide up and down the fretless neck of the cigar-box guitar. The notes wove and blended like pocket water.

"You do know I'm still a child," I said to my father. "An *innocent* child."

"What did I say that was so bad?" my father said to Dox, but it was too late. The image was already having its way with me.

Most days the door to my father's room stays shut. He's like Fritter, except instead of silence, I hear the typewriter going. Its keys plink. Some days it's a downpour. Other days it's a trickle. He keeps a stack of typed onionskin papers in a milk crate beside the desk. When he's gone from the house, I sometimes hold the pages up to a lighter. The words float in the light. I wonder what he'd do if I actually lit the pages on fire. All that work sent to kingdom come.

WHEN I PULL ON THE rope now, Marianne Moore trots over like a horse.

There are ducks gliding down. They skim the river and settle. Others take flight. It's like an airport out here, the comings and goings of ducks. The dog jerks, and I have to hold her with some resistance to keep her from running off. Even though she barely has any teeth left, she wants to tear into them. It's in her nature, and that gives me hope.

"Where's that phone I gave you?" my father says.

"Why?"

"Where's the phone?"

"I thought it was disposable."

"That's not what I'm asking."

"I left it in the truck."

"Don't lie."

"Okay." I pat my back pocket.

"You should take her picture."

"*You* should take her picture."

"I'm serious. Look at her."

I glance over at Marianne Moore. She's a safe distance from us. I put slack in the rope, and her ears perk up. Her head tilts as she stares at us.

"She looks happy," he says.

"She's not happy."

"Yes, she is. Look at her."

"I am," I say. "I'm telling you, she's not happy."

"Not even a little?"

"No. How could she be?"

In a few months, I'll be sixteen, but my body doesn't know it. It's like it stopped in place. I'm still that child my mother last saw. I'm still that little girl watching. I picture something stuck in my mind, playing on a loop.

"You stay here and finish what you started," my father says.

"I didn't start this."

"Don't get smart."

"Where are you going?"

"My feet," he says, and leaves it at that.

I watch my father on his walk to the pickup. He has to go back because he's feeling the pins and needles in his feet again. It's just his guilt. The back of his vest is gray silk. Some creases still shimmer in gashes of sunlight. He stays in one row and never crosses over into another row. He becomes the size of my hand now. I could hold him, if I wanted, but that's not what I want. Marianne Moore starts to take off after him. I clench the rope. When she whimpers, I shush her.

Marianne Moore tries to pull me toward the river. The river is no longer a smear. A good stretch of it is mottled tan like deer fur. For a moment, I think about shooting the river instead of the dog. I look at her. I start going through a list of every word she knows. I don't know why, but I treat them like they're questions.

"Sit?"

Her ears perk up, and she sits.

"Treat?"

She drops to the ground and waits for me to throw her a treat. I feel bad because I didn't bring any treats. Not that she could really chew them anyway. This listing goes on until I can barely speak the last two commands.

"Roll over?"

She does this one easily.

"Stay?"

And now I'm just stuck again.

I'm a wrench in the cogs.

"Stay?"

She tilts her head.

I'm almost sixteen, a young woman, and I haven't started.

Marianne Moore is trying her best to please me by not moving even an inch.

I look at the river. My phone goes off. It's my father.

"What are you doing out there?" he says. "You need to hurry it up. Like chop-chop already."

"I'm just telling her a couple of things before I end our conversation."

"What things? What conversation?"

"She knows a lot of words, so I'm just saying them, okay? She needs to hear them. They need to get out of her."

"Okay."

I wait for him to keep going, but he doesn't.

"Don't you want to know what words I'm saying to her?"

"Not really. There are too many."

"It's probably for the best," I say.

"Your words, not mine."

I slip the red shells into both barrels. The caps have stamped concentric circles on the bottom, where each pin will hit against the center with exact force. I click the neck shut. I aim the gun. The dog smiles at me, I swear. Then I let out a breath and squeeze the trigger.

THE ROPE TAKES OFF AND heads for the river.

The duck I was aiming for, a mallard with a golf-course-green head, coasts over, but it's the tan one behind it that falls from the sky like a bag of mice. Marianne Moore is full throttle going after that one. The rope is still around her neck and dangles behind her in rip-cord fashion. She jumps into the river and works her way over to where the body floats. She clamps down on its neck and turns to see me. I'm standing on the loamy bank, my toes sinking into the mossy clay-and-sand mixture.

My phone goes off again, but this time I don't answer.

I set down everything.

The river gathers at my waist then runs long, sweeping folds down to my ankles. It feels like a fitted dress. I dive in. A layer from below rises and covers my thighs in gooseflesh. My legs start to kick free. Marianne Moore is just a head bobbing in the distant chop. The body in her mouth is indecipherable.

I get closer by putting my face in the water and crawling forward. I can hear my mother at the pool's edge, but I won't open my eyes. I take huge breaths. The river's bitterness slips into my mouth.

With each stroke I'm putting on a new dress that slips from my shoulders.

Marianne Moore jostles the body to get a better hold. She passes me like I'm not there. I turn and tread in place. I think about grabbing the end of the rope as it glides by. I could drag her down. I could make her breathe water. From here, the land-scape is the color of sweet tea. It hurts my teeth to take it all in.

WHEN WE PULL UP IN the yard, Dox and Fritter are kicking at the chickens. They peck their fists down in the grass until I see that they're actually bending over and tying knots in the long monofilament net we sometimes use to fish for bullheads or blue cats. Later, we'll load the mended net in Dox's boat, where, like a bunched taffeta gown, it will catch slivers of sunlight.

Dox waves his skinny pale arms. "Oh, honey, some boy who looked like Andy Warhol came to see you. And in a golf cart, too!"

"Driving around like he owned the goddamned place," Fritter adds, grinning with quiet jolts in his neck, the folds on the back stacked like a pack of charred hot dogs.

My father pretends he doesn't hear. He steps out of the truck and walks into the house without saying anything. He's still mad at me for not putting the dog down. The back of his vest is a Rorschach test. The drenched cloth doesn't shimmer anymore.

I bring out the duck and hold it up for Dox and Fritter's applause, but Dox is the only one who offers any. Marianne Moore jumps up and tries to get at it like the bird's a piñata.

"Damn, girl," Dox says.

"Her or me?" I say.

"Both." Dox touches the hem of my shirt. I feel like I'm wearing the air it's so damp. "Looks like you traveled here from Golgotha."

The duck is going to go good with a ladle of rice, both the wild kind we've been lucky enough to gather nearby and dry out on our own and also the milled and polished kind we'd scrimped to buy in bulk. All of the window dressings throughout the boat-house are made out of the cloth sacks.

I don't go inside to change. It's so hot out anyway. Whatever I'd put on would suck up the humidity. Instead, I walk around the side of the boathouse that sags, past the graveyard of gutted washing machines and the faded-yellow Gran Torino station wagon that got us here years ago, after my mother left us.

The house has two levels and started out as a place for storage before it was renovated so there could be living spaces. That's what Dox told us. Two rooms upstairs and two downstairs, along with a kitchen area, but the renovation took place a long time ago, when Dox was a young man and had helped build it. Now he's ancient.

I look back at the Gran Torino. It sits on warped gray cinder blocks. My cobbled-together dirt bike, what my father calls a *rice burner*, leans against the station wagon's driver's-side door and holds down flush one end of a blue tarp. Marianne Moore won't leave my side now.

"Go on," I say, but she stares at me like I'm crazy.

Behind the boathouse is an offshoot of the river. It's more an in-let with things narrowing. It was once used as a put-in for boats, back when the town was filled with watermen and people who made their living fishing the spotted bottom of the sound. Dox used to joke that there was nothing left in the river to catch. We laughed; my father joined in until Dox needed to say, "Pearl, when your mother was a girl and visited here, she would—" but he quickly stopped himself.

I wanted someone to talk about her. "She would what?" I said.

"Nothing, honey," Dox said. "Forget I brought it up."

I grinned because I thought he was about to tell a joke.

"She would what, Dox?"

But no one would answer me.

A side of the back porch hangs near the water. I sit on the bowed railing and start plucking feathers off the duck. I'm dropping them. They eventually catch on the inlet's film. I could burn the feathers off if I wanted, I suppose. It's better this way. I smile at the thought of the boy. I can't believe he actually came here to see me. *Me.*

I pull at the feathers like they're petals on a flower.

MY FATHER SAUNTERS OUT BACK. He splits wood. It's his peace offering. He gathers up a portion of the cord and carries the bundle inside to get the stove going. His feet must feel better. I'm glad for him.

I crouch near the spigot of the cistern and wash the rest of the clingy down from the duck's rubbery body. Dox brings over an empty paint can filled with chicken of the woods he's found, and I wash those, too. I comb flecks of dirt from the flame-colored fungus.

"You already fish out the heartache?" Dox says. That's his word for *buckshot*.

I run my hand over the side of the bird that's been punctured and dig my fingers in for the flattened metal bits. I can't get to them, so Dox takes out his Old Timer pocketknife and runs it under water before performing fast surgery.

There aren't many holes, and he comments on this, which means I was lucky to even hit the thing. But I'll take it. It's dinner for now.

AFTER OUR MEAL, DOX AND FRITTER commandeer the pickup. Father and son together again. They say there's a stash of plywood they want to nab. I know my father's thinking we could use it to fix the side of the house that's sagging. I'd use the surplus for a second boat, since the one Dox keeps is really more river than wood. My vote, though, doesn't count.

The stash is in a new lot, in one of the large housing developments closer to town. With it getting dark, Dox and Fritter feel like it's either now or never. If they wait any longer, the sheets will be nailed up permanently.

"Then," Fritter says, "it'll be a bitch to take apart."

Back when we first moved here, I was twelve and barely reached my father's chin. We had lost our home by then. My mother had gone away that summer, and my father, shortly afterward, lost his tenure at the college. The few things we managed to salvage from our home we stuffed into the Gran Torino and hit the road. Marianne Moore, of course, was one of them.

• • •

Our arrival here was akin to a homecoming. Dox took one look at me and said, "I know you already." He said he could see my mother before he could see me. All to say, if my father and I wanted, we should stay. I spent that same evening dancing on the pier.

I had even taken off my shirt like the others and grabbed at my smidge of a belly and hula-ed my way back and forth, accompanied by Dox's drunken rendition of "Tiny Bubbles." Dox and Fritter were three sheets to the wind, with my father at the helm of the invisible boat.

The men were whistling like bullets. They left holes in the air for me to fill. I danced within the torn space of their drunkenness. I didn't care that I was topless. My tan chest was flat like a block of ice. The air was one warm breath belonging to another world.

It wanted to eat me up. I wanted it to eat me up.

"*Enchantée*," my father crowed. He had not given up on learning French. I turned away from them all. My mother's memory fell into a pile of shadows next to my shirt. I shook my chest for the river filled with slick bullheads and tricky moccasins. I held my arms out, all sacrificial-like, shaking every limb. The tips of my nipples, tiny as screws, felt stripped and flush against my skin.

It was in one of the motels where we stayed before coming to the boathouse. There was a small pool where I swam. I remember there was this elderly man, too. He came out to sit in a deck chair. He pretended to check his phone, but I knew he was filming me.

I doggie-paddled and put my face in the water. Sometimes I went under completely for the pennies I dropped. I collected them one by one. When I surfaced, the chlorine would sting my nose and I would cough. I played it up. I pretended I was younger than I was. I thought if he could see me this way, struggling and still a child, then maybe he'd stop what he was doing.

He never asked me if I was all right.

I kept staring up at the balcony. Marianne Moore barked. She was trying to get my father's attention, but he was asleep in the room. If I'm being precise, he wasn't asleep exactly. He was inebriated.

The elderly man wore a T-shirt that read WORLD'S GREATEST GRANDPA. I wondered if I reminded him of someone. Maybe I was a granddaughter who lived on the other side of the country, someone he rarely saw.

On the pier, I kept at hula dancing. I smiled until I looked back to find my father's face had dropped to mostly jowls. He regarded me through a squint. I thought he was trying to summon a yell, having to work himself up to do so. I held my arms out and kept at my shaking, pretending I was this happy, that I could be this child for him. Dox and Fritter were both conjuring Don Ho, goading me on, while my father sat off to the edge of us bewildered, as if he were a stranger that had simply happened upon our revelry. As if he had nothing to do with the creation of this girl before him.

SOME DAYS IT'S ONLY a few boiled eggs split four ways. Other days it's a big dandelion salad and fried bullhead catfish netted fresh from the sound. Fritter builds traps for crayfish, too. We gather and gather, and still, it never seems like it's enough.

I have to help Fritter set and empty the traps now because his legs sink the moment he takes the first step in the water. He's gotten stuck more than once in the soft mud near the banks. Once we had to tie a rope around him and then tie the other end to the rear bumper of the pickup. Dox was crying the whole time because he thought my father was going to hit the gas and pull half of Fritter's body off and leave the rest poking out of the mud.

Other days there's simply no food. I've found you can eat the silence that grows inside a house. It gets so quiet I can hear everyone barely breathing, and that's a feast, for sure.

I used to spy on Fritter until I realized all he ever did was paint the same thing over and over. Dox says Fritter is working on a mural, but the landscape has no faces or figures, none that I've been able to see. It's just a solid wall of black paint rising in increments like a river from the buckled floor of his room.

Fritter takes an empty rifle cartridge, the long-range kind he used to shoot during his tours, and holds it flush with the wall. Above it he paints a thin black line. Each line is the exact length of the bullet casing. On his knees, he works his way from wall to wall.

I THINK OF SOMETHING MY mother once told me, when she was explaining a math problem. I didn't know it then, but she was using Zeno's dichotomy paradox as an example.

"Pearl, go to one end of the room and stand there."

I did it.

"Okay," my mother said as she walked to the opposite end, directly across from me. "I want you to try and reach me. But here's the catch. You can only go half the distance toward me with each attempt. Make sense?"

"No."

We both laughed.

"Come this way," she said, like I was in the deep end of a pool again and trying to reach her at the edge. "Now stop there."

I stood halfway from where I had just been. I studied the invisible line from where I was now to where she still was.

"Now go again."

I immediately walked halfway closer and stopped. "I'm almost there." I smiled.

"Almost. Go halfway from there."

I did it and was so close. I wanted to jump into her arms. "I can almost reach you."

"Right, but here's where it gets tricky. You can only go half the distance each time."

I looked down at my feet and shuffled them in place.

"Are you listening to me?"

"Yes."

"What did I say?"

"You said I can only go half the distance."

"Good."

I stopped for a moment and studied her face. It was so serious, like she wanted to tell me something important.

"I'll never reach you."

She smiled. "Good girl. You're right. You'll never reach me."

I WAS CARRYING ONE OF Fritter's empty paint cans I had repurposed into a pail the first time I met Main Boy. He was standing in front a large FOR SALE sign in an open field not even a quarter mile from where we were staying. The pail was already half-filled with cattail roots, and I was going to boil them down until their middles softened, so I could put them in a stew for Dox with whatever Fritter and I yanked from the traps that day.

I crossed a gully grown over with pampas grass and followed a zigzagging line of pines. Wild onions would have been a nice accompaniment, but none were to be found. The trees eventually thinned near the edge of a fallow field. I remember spotting Main Boy where he was and thinking I was a safe distance, like I didn't exist yet in his mind.

Main Boy remained planted in the middle of the field. He leaned against his glittery red golf cart. Once he saw me, though, he started waving and yelling to get my attention. I went from being invisible to something that could be touched. My heart shook like a fish in a net. Perhaps this is why I panicked and ran away. I didn't feel like being gutted alive.

· · ·

At one point, I dropped the pail and didn't go back for it. Later, only when the field was empty and dark, I scavenged the FOR SALE sign. No one needed to be reminded the world could be bought.

I asked my father if the precise term for what we were was *squatters*. He laughed and said, "God no, Pearl, we're all artists here." Then he sat quietly for a moment. He later made the following amendment: "The truth is everyone is a squatter. It's all borrowed. These bodies. Our names. We don't give them back until we've fucked them up properly." He nodded, as if this were the final word on the matter, as if he had done his parental duty.

Main Boy's real name is Mason Boyd, but I can't bring myself to call him that. He's Main Boy. It's meaningless. It fits him perfectly. He wanted to know if I lived nearby, and I shook my head and wouldn't speak. I wanted him to think I was feral. He asked me if I was going to start high school in the fall, and I grunted, which made us both laugh. He pulled his golf cart alongside me as I picked dandelions, pulling them from their roots while saving their buttery-yellow heads.

He said that he was the president of a club that has a pretty big Web presence. That was supposed to mean something. They post lots of videos they've shot themselves. He said I should subscribe to it, as if I could. I told him no thanks. It is only pranking videos now, but they want to expand into videos that teach people how to survive in the wilderness. I ask him what wilderness is left, and he says plenty.

He and his friends think the world is going to get to a point where it will simply fall apart, where we won't have all the amenities we're used to. I smile at the word *amenities*. I ask him what their club is called, but he says it doesn't have an official name. Because it doesn't have an official name, I tell him they should call themselves Flies. He doesn't like that idea. He doesn't think it would look good on a T-shirt.

All boys are flies at some point in their lives. Even my father, even sweet Dox, though I don't hold it against either of them. Boys can't help being flies, just like some girls can't help pulling off their wings so the flies will spend their lives scurrying in circles.

Flies because they talk a lot of shit and love it, especially Main Boy. He might be the biggest prankster of them all. *Flies* because in the dictionary my father owns, a group of flies is called a *business*. I wish I were making that up. I should refer to their club as a business, but that wouldn't be precise. They are flies. Their business is talking shit and shooting things, though not necessarily in that order.

Mostly in the evenings, the flies go out and riddle road signs with buckshot, with shotguns they borrow from polished walnut-and-stained-glass gun cases. The flies talk about going over *there*, like it's a real place. They should meet Fritter. That would be something. They yammer on about how many they would shoot. They can't wait to leave this town. It's like they're on a crash course they think they're going to survive. Their voices stick together and build into something that's just a larger pile of stank. Fritter could set them straight, I bet, if only he'd allow himself to say more.

Up before my father and the others, I went for a walk near the state road. Around the bottoms of old fence posts were shredded labels of High Life. The glass was scattered like seed. The flies say it's all a joke, but then say they want to be ready for an attack, like it's all coming here, to our little speck of the world. It makes me sad, the way they go on. The world doesn't care about us as much as we think it does.

"Target practice now, so it won't be practice later," the flies say.

"Okeydokey," I tell Main Boy.

When I hear this kind of talk, I feel like I'm eavesdropping on their magenta-haired fathers who take heart medicine. Or to those that pass on it so their mistresses can feed them blue diamond-shaped pills. When the flies boast, there's even that same hesitation, like they're trying to swallow it all down.

"COME ON, PEARL," Main Boy says.

"Where are we going?"

"Come get lost with us."

He wants me to hang out, to go to at least one meeting. He says I can help them make more videos. I could be Wendy in this Lost Boys act of theirs.

"Come on," Main Boy says. "They're gonna love you."

"Who's going to love me?"

"Everyone."

I don't care about that. I don't care about that at all.

He gives me a thumbs-up, like he can read my mind, too.

"What?"

He doesn't answer.

He tries to reach out. I brush his hand away, but he keeps at it until he rests his thumb against my bottom lip. He must think I'm stupid. If I were wild, his thumb would be gone by now.

"You could be pretty hot, if you wanted," he says. "Just saying."

I lean back. He keeps his fist pressed in the air, like there's a thick wall of glass between us. I see his lips moving, but I can't make out what he's saying. I feel like making a fist so I can break this fucking glass.

Evenings I trace the horizon with my fingertip. It's just a line where the river and the sky meet. Beyond this river is the sound, and beyond the sound is the ocean. Everything is barely holding on to the next thing. That's what I really want to tell Main Boy. Everything is barely holding on.

Mostly there's only quiet out here, even when Dox is noodling on the cigar-box guitar, his slide fashioned out of a sliced wine bottleneck. He keeps at a song until he stops. He sometimes finishes what he starts, and sometimes he doesn't. It's an unspoken rule.

My mother used to say that poems were never finished, that they were only *abandoned*. I like to take some things my mother said and flip them on their head. For instance, I think all abandoned things are poems. In this way, if this place where we live together is truly abandoned, then we are living inside a poem.

My father says I'm fifteen going on fifty.

MAIN BOY HAS A BRIGHT red plumber's wrench he uses like a gavel. He bangs the side of his golf cart, rattles one of the metal poles that holds up the glittery roof. Some of the shotguns in the back jostle.

"Order," he says. "Order!"

We're in a shed the groundskeeper emptied out so they could play pretend.

The flies, all tall white boys in buttoned-up polos and khaki jogger pants, are poking each other in the ribs. I feel like I'm behind the scenes of some high-end clothing-catalog shoot where the models are taking a quick break. I wish they'd all just shut up and hold their poses again. I like them better when they don't talk, when I don't know what's in their heads.

Main Boy goes through the names of the other flies—Clint, Reese, Everett, Wythe—and in response every one of them shouts, "Here!"—except for Wythe, who whispers through a permanent smirk, "Present," and that garners a laugh.

If they were in a lineup, I wouldn't be able to pick them out, except for Main Boy and Wythe. Main Boy has tangled towhead hair. Dox is right. Main Boy does look like a young Andy War-hol. Wythe has the same clothes-hanger body, but his hair is shaved into a black crew cut, a thick smudge of ink.

They are the sons of land developers and judges who dress up on weekends as Civil War reenactors. Main Boy says his friends are the future leaders of this town. Yet even though they boast of belonging to important families, I just think of them as flies. They're all flies. *Fucking flies.*

When Main Boy finishes taking roll, he looks at me and says, "Everybody, this is Pearl. She lives in the old boathouse."
    "What boathouse?" Wythe wants to know.
    "It's on a parcel of land my dad bought for me."
    When Main Boy says this, their eyes pass over my body.
    "Does your dad know she's there?" Wythe says.
    "No one does," Main Boy says.
    "Good to know," Wythe says.
    The other flies nod. Their eyes graze my shirt and zero in on my nipples. That's all I am, and they keep nodding. I cross my arms in front of my chest. That's when they stare at my fingers. I rub my slender arms. They want me to stroke them again, I can tell. God, they think I'm stupid. I bunch my shoulders and grip at my arms anyway, like I'm freezing. My stomach won't stop growling.

The flies start eating from a tray of sandwiches Main Boy brought for the occasion. It's one of those long party submarines, sesame-seed loaves cut into generous rectangular portions, dripping with Italian dressing. My mouth waters, and I feel like Marianne Moore. Not the famous modernist poet whose work my father used to teach, but our family dog.

The flies are double fisting. They are making a mess with the shredded lettuce and tomato slices that slip loose between each sloppy bite. No one offers me anything. What they drop gathers in the dirt. They kick it around. I try not to stare.

While they're busy eating, Main Boy takes a creased map out of the golf cart and unfolds it by holding on to one corner and shaking the large piece of paper until it opens fully.

"Took this out of my dad's office," he tells them. "A survey of the county."

He says he's going to work for his father this summer. Right now, it's just looking up private easements and deeds for property owners' names, a bunch of busywork, but soon it will be more than that, Main Boy promises. Soon he'll run the whole god-damned company.

Not one of them speaks, because they can't, so I say, "What are all the red Xs for?"

Someone had used a colored pencil to make them.

Main Boy studies the map with narrow eyes, like he's seeing it for the first time. His head of hair is so white, I have to resist the temptation to reach out and stick my fingers in it. I want to pull it apart like cotton candy.

"That's where we live, dumbass," he says to me. "Those right there are our houses."

The flies laugh on cue.

I glance over the map. Now I see what he means. The river is a sinuous line of blue. The clump of red pencil Xs south of it marks where Main Boy and the others live in their behemoth McMansions, though on this map, there's no golf course yet, and no country club. We're standing in a space that's just a big cloud of scuffed vellum.

. . .

I follow the river east to see if he's marked where I live. I find the boathouse. Its structure and the plot of land around it are actually drawn in black ink, there on the original, like I belong in this world more than the flies do.

"Why did you even invite me here?" I have to say.

"I'm getting to that," Main Boy says.

I shift my weight. I can feel the sides of these shoes about to give, the canvas wanting to split near each pinkie toe. The flies watch my feet, then their eyes rise and stop, glued to the sunbleached hairs on my skinny legs.

THEY'RE MAKING A NEW PLAN, and they need someone to watch them make their plan. They don't say this, but I feel it. The map is for finding places to shoot. Once they get a general idea, they'll scout out the location. They're talking like they're suddenly big-shot film producers. They throw around industry terms they read somewhere, and they pause just before they use them. Some wonder aloud if they should be shooting pranking videos or just doing survival videos exclusively, which is Main Boy's vote.

"What's the difference?" I ask.

"Fake blood versus real blood," Wythe says. He sneers.

The others laugh, even Main Boy.

The goal is to get lots of views, to keep being seen.

"We need subscribers," one of them says.

It doesn't matter what comments are posted. The more views and the more negative comments, the better, or the more views and the more positive comments, the better. It's all the same.

Negative and positive cancel each other out.

"Views are views," Wythe has to add like he thinks I'm an idiot.

. . .

Main Boy says they'll get paid once the total reaches into the tens of thousands, but he doesn't know the full details just yet. The others nod like they know, but no one knows. They have their homes with dead bolts on the doors, their dresser drawers filled with folded clothes.

"We just need to post something that'll get their attention," Main Boy says.

"Who are *they*?" I ask.

"What are you, a teacher?" Wythe says, all flat faced, his hair a thumbprint.

Main Boy laughs, but then says, "*Tranquila*."

I don't know if he's talking to Wythe or to me.

The flies make a list. Clint thinks it would be funny if they shoot a video of them blasting all of the speed-limit signs they can find. He pushes on the map. His finger slides over a back road that runs near the river. The flies hover around him.

"That's just stupid," Wythe says. "Something like that won't go viral."

"Sure it will." Clint clutches another hunk of sandwich. He takes a bite and keeps talking. "It'll be so fucking funny."

"Fuck funny," Wythe says. "What we need's a prank that's funny, yes, but that's also scary. People need to click on it and can't believe they're clicking on it. You know what I'm talking about? They need to do it again and again, and even send it to their friends, and then those motherfuckers will be shaking their heads the entire time they're clicking on it, like they can't believe they're doing it, too."

"What do you propose?" Main Boy says, still holding on to the wrench like a gavel.

"A beheading," Wythe says, and looks right at me.

. . .

Wythe takes out his phone and sticks it in my face. The others watch me, even Main Boy.

"Go ahead," Wythe says. "Push play."

I touch the screen.

The landscape looks like another planet. There's a man in an orange suit. He's on his knees. There's a person in a black suit with their face covered in black, the cloth wrapped around and around. I think of Fritter's mural, how if it were cloth, it could be worn like this. The person in black is holding a knife and lifts it up. I turn my head.

"What?" Wythe says, laughing. The flies crowd around the phone's tiny screen, their faces twisting into knots.

Main Boy looks into my eyes. "Sorry," he mouths.

"Fuck you," I say back.

Wythe pauses the video. "Hey, what's your problem?"

"I don't have a problem."

"It's too much for you?"

"I've seen worse," I say.

The flies laugh.

"Yeah, right," Wythe says. "What the fuck have you seen that's worse than that?"

I step back and let them finish the video. I don't tell them about my mother. I don't tell them how she's still in my head.

DURING A BREAK IN THE MEETING, Main Boy holds up one of the shotguns and says he'll teach me to shoot if I kiss him and maybe kiss a few of the others. I tell him he won't have to teach me; if he tries to kiss me, I'll be able to shoot just fine.

He laughs. The flies laugh, too, except for Wythe.

Soon the rest of us are laughing like it's the funniest thing we've ever heard, though I know it's not that at all. I look around. Their fingers are just as messy as their mouths. At one point, it feels like they've all taken a step toward me, like they want me to wipe their mouths for them. Or lick their fingers.

"Why'd you come here?" Wythe says to me.

"Mason kept talking a big game about the club," I say. "I had to see what all the fuss was about."

"So what do you think?" Clint says.

"I think you're pussies, if you want to know the truth."

"Don't hold back, girl," Main Boy says. He grins at the others.

"Don't call me girl."

"Sorry, I was just trying to be nice."

"Maybe we should check," Wythe says, "just to be sure."

"Sounds good," I say. "I'll show you mine if you show me yours." I don't wait. I start pinching at the air.

"What the fuck you doing?" Wythe says.

"Just practicing."

"Practicing what?"

"Trying to grab it."

"Shit," Wythe says, sneering, but the flies are already on him with elbows.

"Burn," they say, "burn."

I go over and climb on my dirt bike. I balance it between my legs.

All of them stop now. Their eyes lock on the bike's gas tank, right where it's touching.

"I thought you were boys, but I should've known you're just flies."

"Pearl, wait," Main Boy says.

I kick-start the bike and pull in the clutch, shifting the gear into first. The bike lurches forward, like it wants to attack whatever is in front of it. I rev it good and loud. The back end crackles. I want it to be spraying glass and shrapnel. Clint and some of the others cover their ears, but not Wythe and Main Boy.

"Head on up to the clubhouse," Wythe says. "Tell them you're our guest."

He nudges Main Boy.

"Fuck all of you," I say.

The bike shudders hard between my legs.

I cross the golf course, but no one follows me.

I tear a line down the fairway and then up onto a green that's so flat and smooth it looks painted on. I burn a donut around the flag, just to do it. When I reach another fairway, I pop a wheelie and keep going. My heart is in my throat. I finally reach that spot on Main Boy's map where the blue line stretches out and curves. It's the river. I don't care what his map says. It's not all his. It just can't be.

IN THE DEEPEST PART OF the river, fish bore through columns and loosen the last of the cold. They carry it on their bodies like little coats. I play my father's shoulders. They thud. Dox jangles and slides on the neck of his cigar-box guitar. Its metal resonator, a perforated snuff-tin lid, vibrates out from the middle.

I join the clipped chorus on "Drown," and once the verse kicks in, we all drop out like emptied crab pots. Fritter is the only one left with his bellow clicking at the end. He scoops us up and pours us out onto a long tabletop like bright red blue claws and butter-yellow corn. It's a down-home boil. We have the rice and some potatoes, but we take a vote and decide to save it for tomorrow. This evening only songs will feed us.

My father dances away, his arms held out all airplane-y as he hits a gust and careens down steps to the start of the pier's warped boards.

"You be careful," I say.

He waves, lifting a wing flap. "You be careful."

The river goes from television static to one smooth brushstroke. My father pounds his boots on the boards. The water below responds with concentric circles around the pilings. Dox starts in on another tune that's meant to be a second course. Fritter goes darker, singing like he's happy-crying at a funeral. It almost hurts to hear him. Because it's on the heels of so much joy from earlier, I feel like we can bear it a little while longer. That's what I tell myself. Just a little while longer, all this living we're doing.

"Goddammit," my father says. "I wish I could take this moment and seal it up for later."

"Like you're canning pickles," Dox says, nodding.

"Like I'm canning some goddamned, motherfucking pickles, yes," my father says, a shell of his professor self. He immediately dives off the end of the pier, headfirst into black water. In an instant, he's Amelia Earhart's Electra over the Pacific, his arms outstretched with rivets and gleam, but then he's gone in a plunk. The air builds with a charge. I can taste it, every shell around every nucleus.

When my father surfaces, he gasps. Dox and Fritter go radio silent. We wait, but my father is also waiting.

"Did you miss me?" He leaves a fan of hair flat against his face. It covers his mouth, like he's talking through a veil.

Sometimes all he wants is for me to smile.

IN ANOTHER LIFE, IT WAS just a secret I wasn't supposed to tell my father.

We're going to wake up early, before he starts his shower, and my mother is going to let me stir the water in with the prepackaged mixture for beignets. I even get to pat the dough flat, so we can then cut them into squares.

I've seen her do it before. We fry up the pieces until they puff up light brown. My mother likes to hold her arm out and say, "When they get this color, we'll know they're done." That's when we let them cool on a plate lined with paper towels, all before we sprinkle them with the confectioners' sugar white and chalky as talcum powder. If you do it too soon, the remnant oil clumps the sugar together and ruins the look.

"Won't this be good?" my mother says, talking about the plan. She nudges me with an elbow. We're thick as thieves, partners in crime. Cut from the same bolt of cloth.

Discussing the future this way makes me happy. I clap my hands but am careful only to make the gesture without really clapping. I don't want to slip and make a loud noise and have my father call out from the other room, "Some of us are trying to read here!"

The next morning, my mother doesn't tell me she's already started the oil. I can feel the warmth coming from the pan. I step back from the stovetop.

"Sprinkle water in it," my mother says. "That's the only way to test that it's ready."

I do as she tells me, flinging a handful, and the oil pops suddenly. It hits my arm. Startled, I scream. My father tears into the kitchen and grabs my wrist and asks what's wrong. He doesn't let go of me, even when my mother says it was just a joke, and my father grimaces and asks me, *me*, "What the fuck is wrong with you? What did you think was going to happen?"

"Leave her alone," my mother says. "You go from zero to sixty, I swear."

Or maybe I have this backward.

When it comes to my mother, I sometimes forget certain details. Maybe it was my father who bought the beignet mix and the confectioners' sugar, and that the two of us had gone to the store with the thought of preparing a special meal for my mother because we never really did that kind of thing for her.

My mother had just passed a series of exams on comparative literature, ones she had been studying for as long as I could recall, and as my father and I are walking the aisles and reading aloud the funny-sounding names on the products lined up in boxes around us, I suddenly dart off and try to hide from him, first at the end of the cereal aisle and then at the end of the juice aisle—he goes one way and I go the other—and I keep going until I find myself near the back of the store. I freeze when I see two people clinging to each other and letting go, like they're practicing a dance.

The woman is holding a bottle of wine and the man is reaching for her other hand. When the woman sees me, she drops the man's hand and turns her face, but I've already seen her. It's done. I don't call out to her because I realize I've forgotten about my father, that I left him a handful of aisles back. I take off to try and find him, and he's there where I last left him, studying a lineup of jarred mustard. I must have this look on my face because when he sees me, he says, "What, you missed me?"

And am I a terrible daughter because at that very moment I tried to rush him out of the grocery store? That I grabbed the basket of things from him and said, "C'mon, c'mon, we have to go," and I let him think it was because there was a show on television that I wanted to watch, and that nothing else mattered in the world to me more than getting home and seeing this show?

There was the fraying conveyor belt at the checkout. There was the growing line of beeps from each scanned item. Fake jewelry made indentations on the cashier's plump pink hands. There was the swipe of my father's credit card, which meant we were almost free to leave. When I turned around, only strangers were milling about the aisles. I smiled then because I could see that where my body had been had been replaced by these other people I would never see again.

My mother was late coming home that night. She didn't say where she had gone, and my father didn't press her for an explanation, or at least nothing that I could tell. I lay in bed and waited to hear any sound at all. I tried to fall asleep to the silence. In the kitchen, my mother shook every pill bottle she kept lined up on the counter.

. . .

Sometimes it hurt to live inside my own room. I had to become a girl under the cartoon-pony sheets with her parents not saying one word to each other. I knew they hadn't fallen asleep. They were probably sitting up in bed, each slightly leaning toward their lamps, marking opposite sides of the room, as they read from things pulled out of their pile of books. I think I slept that night, but I'm not sure. I was still awake when my father knocked lightly on my door and whispered, "Let's make that breakfast, Princess," and I knew he meant the beignets.

He was the one who had heated the oil and said, "Sprinkle water in it. That's the only way to test that it's ready." And after I scream from the oil splattering across my arm, it's my mother who appears in the kitchen and grabs my wrist tightly, like she's holding a bottle of wine by its neck. I want to say something so badly, especially when my father begins to chide her. Instead, I look over at the red-haired woman in the framed print my mother loved. The woman is lifting her skirt. She is kicking up her legs in some old Parisian dance hall, despite the fact that those around her look sullen and tired of their life together.

After my father leaves to teach his classes, my mother and I sit on the floor. My mother scatters mail-order catalogs around us. We don't have the money to buy any of these things, but that's not the point. There are pictures of families where everyone looks happy.

One of the catalogs is from L.L.Bean, I think. There's a river in one picture that blurs into the background. A man stands at the edge of it, dressed in waders, with a fly rod and a creel.

"This fishing pole looks weird." I trace my fingertip around the reel. It could be a strainer for our kitchen sink.

My mother glances over. "That's for fly-fishing."

"*Fly*-fishing?"

"Yeah."

"Why would anyone fish for flies?"

She eyes me. I've disappointed her.

She thinks I'm trying to be funny, but I'm not trying to be anything.

"It takes a lot of practice to cast," she says.

"Do you know how to do that?"

She laughs now.

It feels good to make her laugh.

"My uncle," she says.

"You never talk about him."

"I've told you, you just weren't listening."

"Is he still alive?"

"No, he just passed."

"Passed?"

"He died."

"Oh."

I trace a circle around the metal reel.

"When I was a girl, I would visit him," my mother says. "He had land near a river."

"Like this one?" I point at the page.

"Yeah."

"We should go there."

She laughs, but I can tell she's forcing it now. I feel like I've lost her.

"Can you even imagine your father?" she says. "He hates the outdoors. We'd never hear the end of it."

"So."

"One day, maybe."

I study the picture. The water looks like fog.

"What was he like?" I say.

"Who?" Her eyes narrow.

"Your uncle."

"He was nice. He told dirty jokes. He made us laugh."

I turn a page and count the number of smiling adults.

"So did your uncle teach you to fly-fish?"

"No."

"He didn't?"

"There was a boy I saw. He would stand in the river. I would watch him from my uncle's pier."

I wait for her to keep going, but she doesn't.

"Are you hungry?" she says.

I nod.

"Then let's get you something to eat."

She makes me a grilled cheese sandwich and tomato soup. She cuts the sandwich into four triangles. She holds up one and waits.

"Isosceles?" I say.

"Very good."

She lets me take my lunch into the living room. We sit on the floor and pore through more catalogs. I don't look up at her.

"Who was the boy you were telling me about?"

I feign interest in one of the pictures and pretend like I'm reading the caption. My mother's story is a deer I'm trying not to startle.

"I didn't really know him. He was a kid my uncle knew. I would come out in the evenings to watch the boats go by, and he would be in the water casting back and forth, sending the line out in loops. The loops are what I remember most. Like he was writing in cursive."

I'm studying her face. She seems calmed by the memory.

"I can write in cursive," I say. "I can read it, too."

"Who do you think taught you? But don't brag. It's not a good look on you, Pearl."

After lunch, my mother holds a large pair of scissors and I have a kid's pair that sometimes messes up and sticks. Because the blades aren't sharp, they often fold over the page I'm trying to cut and crease it instead.

"Did I upset you?"

"You didn't upset me."

"Good. It shouldn't have upset you."

"Okay."

She finds a catalog with children my age modeling clothes. "Here, pick out something."

We've never done this, not once.

I shake my head.

"What?" she says.

"Dad says we shouldn't buy anything."

"You don't worry about that. We might be coming into some money."

"You have money?"

"Only for you. You choose whatever you want. You're my daughter, too."

"Okay."

"That's my girl."

I smile. There are a few dresses I like. There's also a pair of cute sandals. I wonder if it's too much. I don't want my mother to think I'm greedy.

"Actually, I don't want anything. I'm good."

"You don't have to do that."

"What?"

"Pretend like everything is fine."

"I'm not pretending."

"No? Then pick something good. There has to be something."

I skim the rest of the catalog, but not for things I missed. I look for the things I think my mother would want me to have, but that's even harder to do.

"What about you?" I say.

"Me?"

I nod.

"I have everything I want," she says.

I feel like I've become my father to her. I'm someone else she needs to deceive.

"If you could be anything," I say, "what would you be?"

"Easy. I would be your mother."

"That's cheating."

"I'm not cheating. I mean it."

"But you're already my mother. You have to be someone else."

"Someone else, or some*thing* else?"

"Okay, something else." The option makes me laugh.

"You want me to be something else?" She reaches for another catalog.

"You said it, not me."

She glances at the layouts. Her face brightens. She drops a fingertip into the middle of a page, pointing to an elderly woman reading in a plush blue chair.

"An old woman?" I say.

"No. I would be that open book."

I WAKE TO MARIANNE MOORE trying to bark. It's already the afternoon. I peek my head out the upstairs window to the front yard, where I find Main Boy standing next to his glittery red golf cart and staring up at the house. His bunched towhead even poofs out at the sides like Warhol's wig. He's also wearing the signature Wayfarers. Main Boy shakes his head at something, or maybe it's nothing.

My father's pickup is gone, but off to the side, the blue tarp has been pulled from the Gran Torino. The tarp covers a tall, rectangle-shaped pile. It's the sheets of plywood Dox and Fritter must have scavenged. Broken bricks hold the tarp at its corners. Main Boy waves me down.

I double up on T-shirts, but my nipples still show. I step around the hanging bedsheet that divides the room and grab a pair of my father's pants from his side. I cinch the waist with rope, and roll up the bottoms. My tan legs are twigs, and my toenails are so dirty they look like I'm balancing bright coins on the ends. I slip my feet into the tennis shoes, but the shoes are just as filthy. I drape my hair in front of me and stuff it inside an old Tidewater

Tides baseball cap I found in the river. I peer into the broken mirror my father and I share.

"Fuck it," I whisper.

"Sorry about yesterday," Main Boy says. "We were being dumbasses."

I stand on the front steps, my arms holding my chest. "That's a given. You didn't have to come out here to say that."

"Yeah?" The yearning in his voice makes me want to puke.

If anyone's a dumbass, it's Main Boy for thinking girls are precious. I have news for him. We're not precious. We're the least precious things in this world.

Boys, on the other hand, are fragile as glass.

"You go shooting last night?"

He takes the cue that we're good for now, at least, and grins. "Hit all the signs on the road between here and the big bridge."

"Post the video yet?"

"Nah."

"That's a lot of destruction for nothing."

He full on grins. "Clint was a fool and didn't charge his cart. We had to leave it on the side of the road. I was thinking about going back for it, if you want to come." He pats the spare battery sitting on the rubber floorboard.

"Why isn't he here?"

"My cart only holds two people."

Main Boy doesn't even try to hide his smile.

"I stink," I say. "Just so you know."

"No shit. You're like Pig-Pen."

"Fuck you, Charlie Brown."

"Okay, if you insist."

I yell for Dox and Fritter, but no one answers. They must have gone with my father on a run to scavenge more things. Main

Boy is studying the blue tarp and wants to know what we're building.

"I don't know," I say, "it just showed up."

"That's not what I asked."

"I don't know. Jesus."

It feels weird watching him take it all in.

"How long you planning on staying out here?" he says.

"As long as we can, I guess."

"You have electricity in there?"

"No. Nothing."

"No running water?"

I look at him and then look down my getup. It takes him a second.

"My dad doesn't know you're here, right?"

I don't say anything.

He surveys the property and this time touches his chin like he's doing some deep thinking. I want to tell him that's the fastest way to hurt himself.

Marianne Moore follows us down the road for a ways, but I can't take it anymore. I yell her name and tell her to get until she gives up.

"Who named her that?" he says.

"My father."

"That's a strange name."

"Yeah."

"I think she needs to be put down, if you ask me."

We both watch her hobble off.

"I'm working on it," I say. "By the by, I was already supposed to."

"Supposed to what?"

"You know what."

I hold my index finger to his face and cock back my thumb.

I pretend to shoot him with it. I even fake the recoil. The scenery around us slides by on an invisible conveyor belt.

"Shit, I can do it for you," Main Boy says, "if you're too scared. My dad made me do it for a couple of our hunting dogs."

"Your flies aren't around."

"What does that mean?"

"It means you can cut the shit and stop being Mr. Man."

He mumbles, "Fucking Pig-Pen."

When we turn onto the state road, I see the first speed-limit sign. There are so many tiny holes. It looks like a dented colander someone would use to strain pasta.

"That your work?"

"Mine and Wythe's."

"What did you use? There's still some sign left."

"A four-ten."

"Peashooter." I spit.

"If you say so."

WE KEEP TO THE SIDE of the road because the stretch is 45 mph with a series of blind curves. Main Boy starts whistling, letting his free hand become an airplane that glides up and dips down and back up again. His new polished white Nikes on the one pedal are pushed flush to the floorboard, the spare battery still somewhat between us. I don't say anything about how he seems truly lost in thought. I don't even know if he has that ability, or if there's any sincerity in him at all.

The river is on our left. I let my mind drift. There's a sailboat way past the cruising skiffs. I take them all in. These are the boats my mother loved. The sailboat's curved sheets are taut with wind. When we approach the next sign, Main Boy lets out an honest-to-God laugh.

"Who did that?" I say.

"Clint had his daddy's twelve-gauge. Two shots in it. It was the second one that blew it off the post. It would've only taken me the first try, just so you know."

"You think you can really do it?"

"Hell yeah, my daddy's twelve-gauge would've shredded that sign."

"I'm not talking about the sign." I look at the river.

"Your dog?" He nods.

"That's right. Marianne Effing Moore."

He laughs. "What's the *F* stand for?"

"France."

"Really?"

Main Boy is such a dumbass.

Clint's orange golf cart is angled near the ditch, like it was on a crash course straight for the muddy bank, before it ran out of juice. I jump in the front as Main Boy switches out the battery with a few twists and pats the back of the seat for me to take off. I slam the pedal to the floor and make a hard left turn onto the paved road. I don't see the oncoming car until it's too late.

I TURN THE WHEEL a hard right and run up a grass embankment. The black Honda skids and takes out Main Boy's golf cart. The air is burnt rubber and smoke. A woven basket wedged in the back of the cart goes flying. Tupperware containers pop open. Loads of red sauce and spaghetti splash the pavement. I smell fresh gas. There are napkins that flutter now. I hate that I even see them as wings. They're just napkins. The shattered end of a champagne bottle stabs the rest of the scene. The black Honda keeps on going, but everything around it slows. The brake lights vanish into the car. Grass and swaying branches pull into the red glow that snuffs out. It's all silence now, everything cinched together.

When I spot Main Boy on the ground, I scream. The world opens up again. The edges of glass cut with bright green light. A bass line fades. There are little holes in the way I'm thinking about this moment. Things have jarred loose. I know it's Main Boy on the ground, but I don't want to think about it just yet. When the wind comes back and fills the trees, it sounds like someone shaking a bottle of pills in my face.

MAIN BOY GETS UP AND dusts himself off. His Wayfarers have managed to stay on his nose somehow. A blade of grass is in his hair, but that's it.

"Did you see that asshole?" he says. "He must've been going ninety."

"That was crazy."

"You can say that again."

"Are you all right?"

"I would be, yeah, if people respected the goddamned speed limit."

I hide a smile, though I'm shaking.

"What?" Main Boy says.

"Nothing."

"I didn't get hurt."

"It's not that."

He grins. "What is it then?"

"Please stop talking."

"You thought I got hurt? You know what that means."

"It means nothing."

"Just for a second, you missed me."

"You're crazy."

He laughs, but there's no one there to join him. "I can see it written all over your face, Pig-Pen."

I lean close to him. "There was nothing to miss."

He uses his Wayfarers to lift the hair away from his face. The flecks in his beige eyes look like midges I sometimes find wriggling on the river's surface, just before a fish rises to gulp them down.

He has no good comeback.

We get in Clint's cart and go back the way we came. I drive now. I avoid looking over at the river. We don't comment on how Main Boy had, for whatever reason, brought a basket of food and even champagne.

We find the speed-limit sign lying in the grass.

"Will your dad be mad at you?" I can't imagine what a tricked-out golf cart like that must cost.

"For what? Why would he be mad? Insurance will cover it."

"Insurance?"

"Yeah, you know what that is, don't you?"

"I know what insurance is."

"What is it?"

I channel my father. "It's a racket."

"Yeah, until you need it."

NOT LONG AGO MY FATHER told me a story involving the French poet Paul Verlaine. My father had found it in some of my mother's handwritten notes. Verlaine's mother kept her two stillborn children in pickling jars in her bedroom. She wanted them close, never wanted to let go of them. The young Verlaine must have grown weary, perhaps even jealous, of his mother's obsession, for one day he went into her bedroom and smashed each jar on the floor. When my father finished the story, he laughed and could barely catch his breath. "Some mothers are just fucked-up," my father said. Dox pretended not to hear. I could only picture the babies on the ground, their dead weight covered in glass.

WHEN WE PASS THE SPEED-LIMIT sign that looks like a colander, Main Boy says he forgot something at his house. We need to go there before he'll take me home.

I lift my foot off the pedal and we coast to a stop. I know he's full of shit, but I still ask, "What did you forget?"

"My gun."

"Your gun?"

"Yeah."

He jokes that he wants to be ready in case we get ambushed by a bunch of terrorists.

"You know," I say, "I was just kidding about Marianne Moore."

"Who's Marianne Moore?"

We backtrack for miles. After a while, he points at the turnoff for the golf course, like I can't see the imported palm trees wrapped in decorative lights. We're quiet as we pass the bubbling faux-marble fountain and enter through the lit gates. I remember the donut I left on one of the greens out in the distance. I smile. A paved, lava-smooth path winds us through tall cypresses. It takes us a while to navigate the mishmash of scenery. All of it is supposed to signal something, but I can't for the life of me think what it is or where I'm supposed to be.

From this path we can see into the back of every house we pass. I feel like I'm on a set, behind the scenes of some movie about bored rich kids. Most of these homes have clear bay windows with no shades. In one I see a room filled with silvery items, a gilded-framed painting with its own soft lighting.

Main Boy swipes at a screen on his phone and we enter through an unlocked door on the side of the garage. The garage is so spacious my breathing almost echoes. The floor is smooth and sanded, with no oil stains, no warping. You could fit where I live with my father and Dox and Fritter on just one side of the garage. On the other side, you could put the river and a few home-made boats.

"Come on," Main Boy says, and I follow him inside the house. He saunters down a hallway lined with hip waders hanging above a row of mud boots. He's like a little prince that's returned to the kingdom he'll inherit. When I see the artwork, my chest warms. Somber-toned paintings of pheasants are on the wall, and off to the side, wooden pegs hold heavy coats and red-checkered hats with lambswool flaps for the ears.

On the next wall over is a series of more paintings: *Brook Trout, Brown Trout, Rainbow Trout.* The fish are brighter than any I've ever seen in real life. For a moment, I feel like I've stepped inside one of my mother's L.L.Bean catalogs.

I remember once pretending I was one of the models. She was dressed in a heather cable-knit sweater and cupping a mug of perfect cocoa. She was smiling dreamily at her husband, clad in a matching sweater. I hadn't thought it through to where their kids were. Maybe they were smart and didn't have any. I imagined my husband on his way, just a few pages over, to where he would have his pick of lavish sports gear. Nights when my parents fought in their bedroom, usually over money and the bills beginning to accrue, I would sometimes fall asleep dreaming of the fish my fake husband and I were going to catch together. It was going to be a good life, if I could help it.

WHEN MY FATHER WAS STILL a professor at the college, I once asked him if he would teach me to fly-fish. It was shortly after my mother told me the story about her uncle and the river. I'll never forget how my father answered me. He didn't come out and say he thought that stuff was too expensive. What he did, instead, was put down the anthology he had been scanning, reviewing what he'd cover in his poetry lecture that evening. He started patting his speckled tweed coat, then checked the matching vest he wore with it back then. Each of his touches made his eyes jump.

He acted truly surprised to find every pocket empty of money. He even giggled at the same time, too, which, when I allow myself to think back on it, sits wrong with me. I've always thought of him as possessing a penchant for cruelty, but only with those he loves.

My mother was trying to decipher her dissertation notes. She was preparing for her defense and couldn't be bothered with us. She had been translating the poems of Paul Verlaine and Arthur Rimbaud. The *bâtards*, she called them. Any scrap of paper she found she covered in poems, even the backs of envelopes from medical bills, of which there were more and more. I knew this because whenever one used to arrive, my parents would argue. But now the bills weren't bills anymore. She didn't seem to care about them as much. She would hold them up and recite translations she had written in French. Her cursive I could usually read, but not when it was in another language.

I wish my father had just admitted he didn't know how to cast a fly rod, or to do anything remotely physical, for that matter. Or that on his professor's salary, we didn't have the money budgeted for such a hobby. But he didn't. He just kept playing his body. He drummed the empty pockets, making himself laugh. I felt sorry for him. No, that's not quite right. I felt sorry for myself. I was the daughter of a fool. When I could take it no longer, I stood up and walked away.

To his credit, he immediately stopped, though he had already shown me he was the kind of person who needed an audience, who needed people to view him in a particular light. My father implored me several times to come back and listen to his explanation. It felt good to have a choice I had created, to have this man want something I wasn't going to give.

I disappeared down the hall of our little white shotgun-style house. I walked onto the broken sidewalk. Four more blocks and I would arrive on a manicured college campus. Packs of students were howling at one another between classes, thrilled a weekend of parties and general mayhem was upon them.

My father called me back into the house. In my mind, I was gone. I was walking the campus. I could clearly make out the geometries of land bunched with glowing flowers and green grass. The terrain was shorn and chemically treated. Each square of grass was like a little prison. I kept going, drifting. I wouldn't turn around. He stomped out onto the porch and huffed a few more times, but I was already years younger, sitting quietly on a stool in a bright pink-and-blue classroom.

ALONG THE WALL WERE WOODEN shelves of identical size, stained a radioactive lime hue. Each cubby was filled with baton-size crayons and equally colorful plastic lunch boxes with graphics from television shows like *Dora the Explorer*, *Powerpuff Girls*, and the *Power Rangers*. Inside the lunch boxes were sugar-dusted snacks and wrapped peanut-butter-and-jelly sandwiches with the crusts cut off. Taped to each shelf were the names of every child in my kindergarten class.

I remember my teacher calling for me. "Pearl? Pearl?" She was trying to get my attention, but I sat there on a stool and continued to search for my name. I wanted to see it written among the others. That was important for me, to see I had a place just like they did.

"Pearl?" she said again, standing over me now, and I recall recoiling at her sudden swaying presence, draped as I was in her shadow. When she grabbed my wrist, I would not look up. And when she pulled on my wrist, yanking me from the stool, I kept staring at the names. The children in my class laughed nervously.

I fell to the floor and let my arm stay raised, as if I knew the answer to some other question. Surely it was not to the one my teacher had asked—"Pearl? Pearl?"

I let my weight slip to the bottom of me. My teacher must have sensed the increased resistance. She must have taken it as an attack on her, for she pulled my wrist—there is no other way to explain it—as if it were a handle on a pump and she was thirsty. But no water came. She kept yanking and pushing down on the handle, but still no water. I wasn't going to cry.

My body slipped lower and my wrist lifted higher until I felt my shoulder give. Then, and only then, came the tears. It was the water this woman had wanted all along. Sometimes I think this teacher was my mother, but I know that can't be true. My mother would never do such a thing.

MAIN BOY AND I STOP in front of a study. Brown leather couches are on either side of the room, framed by forest-green curtains that hang from ornate bronze curtain rods engraved to look like bark. It's the floor that startles me. It's an even spread of thinly glazed muted-pastel pebbles. I take one step inside. I close my eyes. When I open them, I'm standing in the middle of a mountain stream. The only thing missing are speckled trout.

"And that's my father's baby, right over there." Main Boy points. A fly rod hangs on the wall. I walk over, slowly. I feel like I'm meeting a movie star. The artist's name is stenciled in cursive near the immaculate cork handle. The cursive makes me think of my mother as a girl. She's sitting on the pier. She's watching loops unroll across the sky.

The rod itself is a piece of art. It's so beautiful. Wrapped around the metal guides are bands of red silk thread layered with clear laminate. I don't dare touch it, though I want to trace my reflection trapped in its polished reel.

Main Boy grabs my wrist. "What are you doing?"

I jerk away. "Don't grab me."

"Then don't try to touch it."

"I wasn't."

"I could tell you were."

"You're wrong."

Main Boy tells me he's never even stood as close to it as we're standing to it now. I feel bad because he thinks he has to lie to me. He's not the only one.

MAIN BOY'S BEDROOM IS OVER the garage. Everything here belongs to him. The room has a high cathedral ceiling because of the steep pitch of the roof, and a pair of curved skylights, each one the length of a canoe. I'm in a church, except I've never been in an actual church.

"Are you hungry?"

"No." I try not to grab my stomach.

"Well, I could eat."

"Okay. I could, too, I guess."

"Good. What do you want?"

"I'll take anything. It doesn't matter."

"Define anything."

"I don't care. Whatever."

"Define whatever."

"Stop being a dick."

"Define dick."

Main Boy takes off down the stairs. I hear him yelling, *"Estrella,"* and saying that he's hungry. I look down at the floor, embarrassed for him. That's when I see my shoe prints. Every step I have taken is on the room's plush white carpet. It's evidence I was here.

IN ONE CORNER RESTS AN acoustic guitar cradled on a stand, its fretboard a swirl of elaborate pearl inlay. The body of the guitar floats in the air. I grin, picturing Dox strumming this immaculate instrument. In another corner is a television monitor the size of a sheet of plywood. It is just as long and flat. Underneath the monitor are three different gaming systems, each one lit and lined up, with a number of jewel cases stacked on the floor. Off to the side of the cases are an open laptop and a few video cameras on tripods. There's also a stand with mounted lights, the huge canister types that would be used on a stage. Maybe it's me, but one of the cameras looks like it's pointing right at his bed. All thoughts as to what this might mean fall away when I spot the open door to his private bathroom.

A huge, gleaming showerhead is surrounded by clear glass walls. Next to the shower is a Jacuzzi-type bath. The tub looks like the bottom of a giant clamshell. I think I'm in love.

Main Boy comes up the stairs carrying a silver tray of sliced meats and bright orange and creamy white cheeses. Everything is rolled and pierced through by toothpicks with crinkled red plastic on the ends. I take a handful and just start inhaling.

"Slow down, Pig-Pen. You'll choke."

"Does that shower work?" I say between bites.

"Yeah."

"Do you mind?"

"What?"

"Do you mind if I take one?"

"Right now?"

I nod.

"I don't mind." Then he smiles. "Can I take one with you?"

HE TAKES OFF HIS SHIRT. His chest is slender and pale, but under his neck there's a rash of color, like it's been scrubbed with sumac. "I'll go start it for us," he says.

I grab more of the food and try not to eat it too quickly. It's hard because I can't seem to chew fast enough. I barely even taste it.

Main Boy disappears around the corner. There's the sound of water.

I wonder how long I can remain a secret, living out where I do.

I take off my shoes first and immediately grimace at the funk of my body. I pull off my ball cap and fan the air. My hair doesn't move it's so full of grease. The belt I had cinched and knotted takes the longest to remove. It drops to the carpet and spirals slowly like one of Fritter's dreadlocks.

"Where are you, girl?" Main Boy says.

I cup my chest, but it's pointless. I don't have anything. I let my arms drop. I'm still that younger version of me dancing on the pier. Nothing has changed in the years since. My nipples are the only things starting to look womanlike, and even then, that's pushing it. They have spread, yes, the center of each one slowly filling, but most everything else is kaput.

I look around the room.

I can already feel the water, its beautiful burn.

I wonder what my mother would say, if she could see me.

I wonder if I've forgotten the sound of her voice.

I try to remember. I close my eyes. Some things just won't come back.

"Are you still there?" Main Boy says again, but it could be my body talking to me, or me to my body. And here, at least, was this chance to pretend. I wasn't going to drift. I was here, in this enormous house, with a boy waiting for me to answer.

How difficult could it be, to pretend?

I pull off my shirt.

"It's okay," I tell myself. "You can do this, Pearl. You can do anything."

IF A BODY IS ABANDONED, does it become a poem?

EVEN THOUGH WE KNOW IT isn't true, Dox says that he delivered me with the help of an alligator midwife, that my first blanket was a patchwork of muskrat pelts, the seams held together with sun-dried honey. He says he wrote a song the day I was born, and he taught it to the bobwhites and the orioles. If I listen up, I can still hear traces of my birth song in woodnotes, though he admits these random birds were terrible students. He sounds like my father and destroys the dream.

I was in the kitchen helping my mother make a salad to go with the marinated kebabs that were cooking on the grill. We had gone to the farmers' market in our little downtown. She said we could buy whatever we wanted. We had bought lettuce, cucumbers, and tomatoes. She was showing me how to slice them with my fingertips bunched up in a certain way so that I wouldn't cut myself. "Let's no one get hurt now," she would say. I took great care slicing the cucumbers.

My father was on campus for the spring commencement ceremony, and we knew that he would soon be returning home, dressed in his black robe and crushed-velvet striped regalia, looking like the other faculty in attendance. My mother and I were ready for him to walk through the door so we could make fun, calling him an emperor penguin or some such, but as he stomped onto the porch, ready to give a quip about the ceremony, the phone in the kitchen rang. My mother picked it up, maintaining her smile, as if to say to me, "You still give him hell, Pearl." I was happy to do so, but as I watched her listening to the caller, I could see the edges of her mouth begin to fall.

My father walked in the house at that moment. He was watching her, too. My mother brought her hand up to her hair, as if the bun had come undone. She turned from us and, while still on the phone, walked into the other room. When she came back, she was her old self, pleasant to a fault.

My father had to ask because he needed to know. He was insistent. She said she would tell him later. I didn't dare say a word, but my father, like I said, couldn't help himself. He asked again. She tried to speak in code on my behalf, but he wasn't having any of it. Even I understood it was news she had been waiting to hear, but that it wasn't the results she had expected.

My father finally took off his black mortarboard and tassel. He must've realized he wasn't going to get a laugh from us now. My mother picked up the knife and began to cut the rest of the tomatoes. She didn't bunch her fingertips like she had just taught me to do. I watched even though I knew what was going to happen. The blade went so deep it must have touched bone. She didn't flinch. I must have been staring because she just turned to me and said, "Look away, Pearl. I don't want you to have to see any of this." But I couldn't look away.

It was later when my father told her he had been invited to a conference. But he also said he didn't have to go. It was on the West Coast, after all. I listened to my parents through the bedroom wall we shared. He was saying he would cancel the trip, and my mother told him, "Don't be stupid. You spent a lot of time on that paper."

"Not as much as you have with your boyfriends."

"Boyfriends? You mean Rimbaud and Verlaine? Is that what you call them?" She laughed.

"Whichever one threw his infant son against the wall."

There was a pause.

"You were listening," my mother said. "I could kiss you right now. Do you know that?"

IN THE MIDDLE OF THE NIGHT, I heard them again.

"I can't keep saying I'm sorry," my mother said. "I can't do that."

"Maybe you can get another test."

"I'm done with pills. I'm done with tests."

"We should know everything."

"That doesn't mean anything. They put a fucking needle right here. I think we know."

"Okay."

"I watched it go in. You didn't watch it go in. I watched the fluid come out."

There was a long pause.

The silence was like a bubble in my chest.

"I don't want to do this anymore," my mother said.

"You're not yourself. You haven't been yourself in a very long time."

"Fuck you."

They started to argue. I wished they would stop, but they couldn't help themselves. I don't think she told him her uncle had died.

There was more I didn't know about either of my parents, but I was used to that. It didn't matter what I knew.

Marianne Moore lifted her head off my leg and looked at me.

"I know," I told her, but I didn't know.

AFTER WE SAW MY FATHER off at the airport, my mother didn't drive us home. She said if my father was going on a week-long trip, then we could do the same. She let her arm float outside the window. The trees and the road signs and the towns we passed that day all looked like they could have been painted on a long sheet of butcher paper. Someone was cranking a wheel and winding the long roll like a stage prop. It felt real and unreal at the same time. I found a station that played Top 40 music, but the knob of the radio wouldn't stay still. There was a wash of static every time we hit a bump in the road. Voices kept trying to come through.

We passed empty fields with FOR SALE signs in their middle.

"Let's play a game," my mother said. "Name your favorite animal."

"That's easy. It's Marianne Moore."

As if on cue, Marianne Moore slipped her head between us and tried to lick our ears.

"I was going to say it was *you*." My mother squeezed my arm. "You're my favorite animal, Pearl."

"I'm not an animal."

"We're all animals."

Outside the station wagon, the air was woven with brine. We stretched our legs and arms. This body of water, my mother explained, was called a *sound*. We pulled into a parking lot buffered with chunks of jagged concrete hauled in from somewhere. The water lapped in crevices like Marianne Moore drinking from her bowl. Disappearing into the sound was a long pier with people gathered at the far end.

Marianne Moore, meanwhile, spun in the backseat.

"C'mon, Princess," my mother said.

I wasn't sure if she meant me or if she meant the dog.

It was one of her jokes. She would call us from another room in the house—"Princess! Princess!"—and wait to see which of us would come running. It made her clap every time to see our stunned faces.

"I got her," I said.

"Can you handle her alone?"

I snapped the leash onto the collar, and Marianne Moore took off, tugging to a standstill. "I guess we're going out there."

All of the benches along the sides were splattered with paper-white gull droppings. Everyone gathered in a circle. Marianne Moore kept pulling, digging her claws into the salt-treated boards.

In the middle of the circle, a man was holding a long knife. He crouched. The others swarmed around him.

"They must have caught something," my mother said.

Marianne Moore looked back at us and started hacking. Nothing came up. She went back to pulling on the leash.

"Go," my mother said, "before she kills herself."

She shooed us both ahead.

The man, it turned out, was younger, more boy than man. His cheeks were brushed with fresh pimples. Near his boots was a large stingray the size of a welcome mat. The top of the stingray was dark brown, and when he flipped it over, its belly was white as milk.

The circle opened to let us inside. I had to jerk Marianne Moore back.

The boy stepped on the barbed tail and pressed a palm onto the creamy flesh.

"What's going on?" my mother said, coming up behind me. "Oh, Pearl, look at that."

The boy said to no one, "Check it," and took his free hand and tried to slip his fingers into the gill slits. The stingray arched and splashed back flat again.

The boy moved both hands to its middle. "I feel something."

He could've been talking to Marianne Moore. I had to hold her by the collar.

The boy sliced the base of the stingray's tail. It wasn't a clean cut. He had to press harder to get through the last bit of cartilage. I felt it crunch. My body went cold.

"Let's go," my mother said, touching my back, but I didn't move. I watched the boy. I was held as he stabbed the knife into the pier. He placed both palms flush against the belly.

"Well, would you look at that?" my mother said.

A baby stingray slipped out. There was a collective gasp. The boy took the little diamond-shaped body and dropped it in the water.

More baby stingrays appeared from the mother. They followed the path of sliding out of her. The boy began to fling them like cards. My mother's hand trembled against my back.

"Stop that." Her voice rose. "What are you doing?"

The boy froze and looked at her. The circle quickly split and spilled behind him. Another baby stingray slipped into his hand. For a moment, I felt sorry for the boy. He held the small body up and offered it to my mother.

"It's just a baby," she said. "Don't you realize it's just a baby?"

"I'm saving them." The boy shrugged.

He placed the baby stingray in her hands.

"Take it back!" She held it out to him, but the boy was already busy dragging the mother.

"Please," my mother said, crying now.

It shocked me that she was crying.

The boy took the baby from her hands. He threw both of them, the baby and the mother, over the edge. I turned my head.

When he picked up the mother's severed tail and held it in the air like a stick, I thought Marianne Moore was going to lose it for sure.

WE TELL NO ONE. Mason Boyd becomes my secret, and I become his. He says that's the way it has to be, if I want to keep living where I live, that is. "My dad doesn't need to know about you and the others." He says this a lot.

I like being with him, so I don't argue. After all, if we didn't have the boathouse, where would we go? Where would Dox have another pier to sit out on and play his cigar-box guitar? Where would Fritter be able to finish his mural?

Where on earth would my father be able to keep me this safe?

I show up after Mason's parents have left the house for the day, his father in a white Ford custom F-350 diesel truck and his mother in a sparkling-champagne Mercedes SUV. When they're gone, it means we can spend all of our time holed up in his room. We do it four times, sometimes five times even. He calls me a rabbit, but it's more like dams have broken inside us and the rivers are finally running wild. We're just forcing away the sediment that had gathered in that one spot for too long.

We're just being ourselves is what I want to tell him.

Mason likes to pull up video clips on his laptop and we try to reenact some of them. It always ends with us in the shower, like we're trying to wash it off, but then he wants me to go down on him, and I say, "Only if you do, too," and he nods and then pushes my head down. When he finishes, he never goes down on me, even though I'm in the shower with him, glazed with the same water, my body the cleanest it's probably ever been in my life.

When I ask later why we can't hang out in other parts of the house, where he tells me there's a Ping-Pong table and even an enclosed racquetball court in the basement, any place other than his room is really what I'm asking, Mason shrugs and says, "If you don't want to be here, then fucking bolt," but I don't care how it sounds, I want to be here. I need to be here.

If we had a map stretched out, I would push on this one spot. Right here. And I tell him that, I want to be here, and that makes him smile. If I was being precise, I would tell him how I want to lie in his bed, on sheets I didn't have to scrub, and I want to feel the cool air of the AC slip into the room unannounced and cup my face and make my nipples sharpen as I stare up at the pair of skylights floating on the ceiling and think this isn't such a bad life, having everything you desire right at your fingertips. I would tell him to forget what he knows, that, yes, we're out there on the property his father bought for him, but that doesn't mean we have to leave. No one needs to know we exist or ever existed. I would tell him, as long as I could help it, I'm not going anywhere, and isn't that what we're talking about here?

AFTER I HAD COME HOME from that day in kindergarten, my father had sworn never to send me back, but that was just talk. My parents fought because my mother thought I had made up the story, and it only infuriated my father even more, especially since my shoulder had almost been dislocated. "Why would she lie?" my father said, but my mother wouldn't answer.

The next morning, while my father walked to campus for his office hours, my mother didn't put me on the bus. Instead, she drove me to the doctor for an exam. The doctor was an older Filipina woman who had long slender fingers just like Dox, though I was a lifetime away from meeting Dox.

The woman gently touched along my shoulder.

"What do you think?" my mother asked the doctor.

"If you care about this little girl, you need to leave him."

I **WAKE UP AND CHECK** the traps for crayfish. I hoist the soaked lines and raise the chicken-wire cylinders to scrub the sides glazed with mud, but nothing is in the middle of the traps, one after the other, except for emptiness. Fritter stays in his room and so does my father. Only Dox is awake and in the sweltering kitchen, cutting the eyes out of a few potatoes soft as hacky sacks. His cigar-box guitar sits over in the corner next to Marianne Moore, who's panting like she's huffing Freon. I haven't heard Dox play in a while, but I don't mention it so as not to stir up anything.

"Honey, where you been going?" Dox says without looking up, his gray hair a chunk of marble chiseled into the texture of lambswool.

"Nowhere."

"Is that right?" He says it like a question he doesn't expect to have answered.

"I'm just riding."

"Riding what?"

He doesn't look up. He keeps cutting out the eyes.

"My bike."

"How much gas does that bike of yours hold?"

"I don't know. A lot, I guess."

"You riding far out?"

"Why are you asking so many questions, Dox?"

"Just checking on you. I don't want you getting too far away and run out of gas and can't make it home to us."

"I'd find my way back."

"On a golf cart?"

I don't answer him because I love him. Dox, that is.

I walk outside and get on my dirt bike before he can stop me, but when I turn around, no one is standing there. There's just the boathouse with its side sagging, its broken washing machines in the yard. Marianne Moore is nowhere to be found either.

I rev the engine and lift my feet off the ground. The scenery moves on its conveyor belt. The bike is on automatic. It pushes onward, like there's a homing device that will carry me safely, unharmed, all the way to Mason Boyd's bedroom.

I lean into it and let it take me.

REESE IS STANDING ON THE highest branch of an oak and tying off climbing ropes and carabiners.

"Does he know what he's doing?" I say.

"No clue," Mason says.

"Then why's he up there?"

"Short straw."

"Well, that's real smart."

Wythe sidles up next to me, holds his waist where a belt buckle would be if he were wearing one. "Howdy, Fuckface."

"Really?" I say.

Mason is suddenly deaf.

Everett is helping Clint into a harness.

"You guys climbing the tree, too," I say.

"No," they both chime.

Fucking flies.

"We're going to make an obstacle course," Wythe says.

"In the tree?" I say.

"Part of it."

"That seems excessive."

"What does?"

"Your stupidity."

Wythe fumes.

"Can you film us?" Mason says, suddenly alive.

"Sure," I say. Behind me is their fleet of tricked-out golf carts, minus Mason's.

"We'll all get up in that tree in a second."

"And then what?"

"Then you take this camera and film us."

"Then what?"

"What do you mean?"

"What are you going to do in the tree?"

Wythe leans in and punches Mason in the arm. "I told you she wouldn't get it."

"I'm just trying to understand why I'm here," I say.

"You're here," Mason says quietly, "because I invited you. If you want to go, just say the word. Just say you'd rather be somewhere else."

Wythe won't look me in the eye. He's too busy staring at my neck.

"I'll do it," I say.

"Fuck yeah, you will," Wythe says.

THAT NIGHT, MY FATHER STOPS me on my way to bed. He holds up his arm and taps the scratched face of his wristwatch, making a big show of it. It must have been annoying to be one of his students.

"She's still alive," my father says. "Just so you know."

"I know she is."

"So we'll just let her keep on living?"

"She doesn't get to die. Not yet."

He makes a kissing noise, and Marianne Moore comes from around the corner. She's dragging one of her hind legs until she catches her balance and hobbles, but then lifts the paw again and freezes.

"She's favoring it," he says.

"That's one interpretation."

"How much more evidence do you need?"

"How much more what now?"

"You heard me."

"You make it sound like a crime."

"Keeping her alive, yes. Putting her down, no."

"I would reverse it."

"Pearl, you can't go holding on to things."

"I thought that's what we did."

"Not when you really, deep down, know you should let go."

I laugh, but he doesn't flinch.

"She's not well, Pearl. She hasn't been well for a long time."

"She's fine. Here, girl. Come here, girl."

I make the same kissing noise as he did, and the dog struggles to get closer to me. When she does, she leans all of her weight right up against my leg. If I take a step, she'll crumple to the floor for sure.

"So that's what fine looks like." My father gives her a once-over and nods. "Okay. Good to know."

"She's not ready."

Both of my legs hurt from riding the bike back and forth to Mason's house. My wrists and arms, too. I rub the ash from my knees. I want to sit down on the floor with Marianne Moore, but I'm afraid if I do, I won't be able to get back up.

"I think you know she's done." He bends down and rubs the dog's head and ears, and she licks the graying scruff on his neck. The two of them smell the same, like rot. As if reading my mind, my father stares up at me and sniffs the air. "Someone rolled around in flowers."

I shrug.

"That's strong perfume," he says, even though it's just soap from Mason's shower.

"It's not perfume."

"So what's the story?"

My father touches my arm and leaves a mark from whatever was on his hand. I study it and try to rub it off. It's ink or grease. It smears. I should tell him the story Mason keeps telling me, that the land where we live was for sale, that everything around us has been bought. That's what Mason has mentioned a thousand times already.

"There's no story to tell."

"Just like your mother." He laughs. "You and your secrets."

"That shouldn't be an insult."

"Who said it was an insult?"

I sit down in front of him and unlace his boots. It's the least I can do. He is terrible about checking his feet, so I do it for him. He used to complain of pins and needles all the time. He doesn't do that anymore.

I soak his feet in a bowl of Epsom salts and scrub the bottoms real good. The tops of his feet have blown veins and are silvered blue with lavender streaks, like hickory shad pulled from the river. I clip his nails for him and gather each splintered yellow crescent and put it in the coffee can with the other gnarled pieces he seals away and stuffs under his bed. He thinks we're living in an artists' colony. He thinks he's Picasso. When I look up at him, he is crying, quietly.

"Did I cut you too close?"

He shakes his head.

I rub his feet until he eventually conks out. There are a few bright notes being plucked down by the pier: Dox as a presence woven into a fragment of a song. Fritter is a long pause in his bedroom. I leave my father, go downstairs, and stop next to the empty cans of black paint stacked beside Fritter's door. Most of the cans are crusted and sealed shut. I find one can I can open. In it are wet remnants I sometimes use with Q-tips to do my toes or my fingernails. Because my father is asleep now, I do his toes and his fingernails. I don't feel like fishing out the keys from his pocket and starting up the truck so I can charge my phone, otherwise I'd do it and take a bunch of pictures to show Mason later. He'd appreciate this prank. The flies, too. I lie awake in bed and try not to think about the day, and all those bodies swinging from branches.

MY MOTHER AND I DIDN'T speak about the stingray again. Instead, we climbed in the Gran Torino and kept driving until we reached the big bridge. We pulled off into a side lot near the water. There was a park with a wide field and a hospital nearby.

"I think we're close to my uncle's place," she said.

"Can we go there?"

"One day."

Gulls circled overhead. Marianne Moore whimpered. I could just tell she wanted to get out on the grass and show the gulls what she could do. I asked my mother if it was okay, but she didn't answer. She was looking at her hands. I got out and let Marianne Moore go. The dog tore across the field and spun.

The gulls looked pinned to the sky.

I got back inside and sat next to my mother.

"I wish I could be a boat," she said.

We passed more fields with FOR SALE signs.

We drove home in silence.

BEFORE MY FATHER RETURNED FROM his conference, we made a trip back and parked in the side lot near the big bridge. My mother had brought all of her pills with her this time. She lined the bottles up on the dashboard like it was our kitchen counter. When she shook each one, it sounded like rain.

Then she surprised me. She doled out half of the pills and asked me to hold them. We didn't say anything. She poured herself the rest. We both looked at the mounds in our hands. They were so full. I didn't want to spill them.

I sat completely still. I tried not to breathe.

"Do you want me to go first?" she said. "Would that help?"

I nodded, even though that's the last thing I wanted.

I told myself not to cry.

"You're my girl. You know that, don't you?"

I didn't answer her.

She wanted me to watch her swallow all of them, every last pill, and I did. I did that for her. I sat there like a good daughter, like I was the best daughter in the world. My hands were still full. I hadn't moved. I couldn't move. The pills held me in place.

"Here," she said. "Let me take those. You shouldn't have those."

When she finished mine, we held hands. She was smiling.

"You can't leave me," she said.

"I won't."

"Promise."

I waited until she closed her eyes. Then I ran as fast as I could. Marianne Moore wouldn't stay. She chased me all the way through the hospital's sliding glass doors.

I WAKE BEFORE THE OTHERS and gather up more empty cans. I pass new wooden posts spaced apart in the water with the net Dox and Fritter mended. The faint line of the net is stretched out and still. There is no movement around it whatsoever. The morning is birdsong and humidity. The volume on both steadily rises. I wish I had that fly rod. I'd figure out a way to make it work, send a line out, and maybe catch a mess of silver perch. That would be something.

I step into the water, and the brown velvet head of a moccasin peeks up just a tad. It's cruising along, not too far away, on a slight current. It isn't interested in what I'm doing. I let out a sigh after the snake is downriver, then wade out some more and check the first trap. When I tug on the string, I know immediately from its weight. Each one is a little jackpot. Greenish bronze bodies click against one another like a deluge of pennies. I steady the cans for the gush.

On my way back to the boathouse, I spot where the net is because it's moving in quick jolts. There's something in the water, maybe caught up in the net, I don't know. I set down the cans. All of those crayfish begin to mount an escape. They use each other's bodies like ladder rungs to climb. I shake the cans and the crayfish fall back. They pause for a second, stunned. That buys me just enough time to lift an end of the net closest to the water's edge. What rises, wrapped in the lines of monofilament, is the largest blue catfish I've ever seen. It's probably forty pounds. Its head is wide and hard like a football helmet. I undo the other end of the net and furiously yank both ends to shore.

The blue cat thrashes and tangles itself up good. I beach the behemoth in the mud. I don't care that the crayfish have regrouped and are spilling out of the tops of the cans. I've lost half of them, easily. The blue cat starts with its grunting. It sounds like a ratchet tightening on a bolt. I can't drag it all the way back in without tearing up the net, so I loosen one of the posts, working it back and forth out of the mud. Once I free the board, I swing it high above the fish and bring it down on its monstrous head.

I run back to the boathouse. I can't breathe, it's so hot. The air is a dress made of pink insulation. Its splinters catch in my throat. Dox is on the back porch drinking coffee from a tin cup. When he sees me, he holds it up and asks if I want to join him. I wave the idea away. He laughs. I look around the yard and then grab the tarp off the stack of plywood.

"Where you going with my raincoat?" Dox says.

"I'll be right back."

"You better be."

I pull the blue cat onto the tarp, and once its belly is all the way on, it wakes and starts twisting its body, like it's trying to swim upriver to where I've lifted the end of the tarp with both hands and have the bunched material thrown up over my shoulder. I'm hauling a sack of goods that has burst open. All that's left is this ugly forty-pound bottom-feeder. Its gut is probably stuffed with polished beer-bottle shards and used rubbers from the weekend boat parties I sometimes hear out on the river. But I don't care. It's fat where it needs to be. I feel it with every thrust of my body moving forward, with every pull and step I make in the direction of the boathouse.

When I get to the edge of the yard, Dox sees me, drops his tin cup, and runs in the house singing. Out comes Fritter in cutoff beige-and-tan camo shorts and nothing else. All I see are haywire dreadlocks and his bouncing chest. The man has titties, and I don't. The world isn't fair.

The blue cat thrashes to remind me what's what, and I keep pulling the cinched part of the tarp over my shoulder and leaning forward. Fritter finally relieves me, taking the ends from my hands.

I watch the fish swim past me on the flattened sheet, up to the steps of the boathouse. I still think I'm holding it in my hands. I can't unclench my fingers. My father steps out on the porch, dressed in pants and vest only. He starts clapping, and Dox steps out from behind him and does the same. Fritter drops the end of the tarp and looks down and then looks at me and joins them. All three of these men are clapping for me, but my fingers stay curled, like I can't decide whether I want to make a pair of fists.

NEXT TO THE PIER IS a plank mounted along one of the rail-
ings and streaked with tiny scales and dried blood. On one end
of the plank is a long, crooked nail the length of a railroad spike.
The nail points end up. It's snagged a part of the sky.

Fritter uses this nail to impale the heads of fish he cleans by
the water. He lifts up the blue cat and in one swift gesture plops
it onto the plank. Immediately, blood begins to pour from under
its chin.

"Go get the knife," Fritter says to me. "And the pliers. Make
sure to get those."

I go in the kitchen for both and have to rummage around in one
of the drawers. When I come outside, my father and Fritter are
discussing the fish, but then Fritter notices me and takes a big
step away from the railing.

My father says, "It'll be good for you to do this one on your
own. Just in case we're not around."

"I've cleaned fish before."

"Nothing like this, you haven't," Fritter says.

I glare at Fritter. "Whose side are you on?"

"No one's side."

"There are different sides?" My father shakes the idea from his head.

The blue cat doesn't even look real to me now. I poke and push into the slime of its cushioned skin. It doesn't move.

"Run the blade right here." Fritter draws a line with his fingertip.

For some reason, I can't do it. I put the blade up to its skin, but then pull it away. Fritter takes the knife from my hand and slices a horseshoe pattern, starting from one spot just behind its enormous head. He mirrors the cut all the way over to the opposite side. Flies begin to gather.

"At least separate the skin from the meat," my father says to me. "Just slip a finger underneath and move it around a little bit."

It's all papery tissue between the muscle and the skin's slick coating. I make a small space, enough for the ends of the pliers to get a decent hold. I clamp the nose end down and slowly pull back toward the tail. I lift. The slime and the skin come off in wide strips. I keep going.

There are more flies now, a real *business*. They swarm the pale meat, some bouncing off and swirling back to have another run at it. I can tell Fritter had been careful not to put the knife in too deep. He didn't want to ruin it, but the flies are insistent. They cover my hands. They kiss the slime. They plunge through the heat, into the sides of the blue cat. There are so many, they're trying to become the fish's second skin.

My father and Fritter have left me to it. Now they have stepped back onto the porch with Dox running the glass slide up and down the neck. I wipe at my face with the back of my wrist. My hair sticks to my cheeks and chin.

"What are you doing out there?" my father says.

I feel like taking off my shirt and shaking my nipples at them.

The blue cat is covered in so many flies now.

I fan the top of it, but the flies don't move. They know a good thing when they have one.

"Come on, honey," Dox says between riffs.

I'm careful with the side fins, making them retract so as not to get stabbed. I lift the fish off the nailed plank. The wound makes a sucking sound. I cradle the body. I have to keep my footing.

Because it doesn't move, it feels like I'm holding Marianne Moore in my arms.

"What are you doing now?" Fritter says.

"I'm washing it off."

In my mind, there are too many flies. It shouldn't have to be covered in them.

I step off the pier to wade in by the bank.

"There's water in the cistern," my father says. "We'll use that to clean it up. Put it back on the board and pull off the fillets."

"I'll get to that," I say.

"Wait." Dox laughs. "That's breakfast, lunch, and dinner!"

I keep the blue cat cradled to me. There's no way I'm letting go. I carry it off the pier and over to the side. I bend down and dip its body into the river. The flies scatter and don't come back right away. They circle.

Rinsed now, the muscles look brighter. Then all at once the fish tenses, electrified. I can't help it, I scream. It's not my imagination. The fish pulls away from my grasp and slips underwater like a submarine.

HAMMERED FLUSH ONTO FRITTER'S DOOR is a sign carved into a cut piece of plywood. The message reads DON'T EVEN THINK ABOUT IT, but I knock anyway. I hear a low groan and then the door swings open. Fritter's bare chest is large as a bank safe. He smells like my father and Marianne Moore put together. A cloud of turpentine rushes out from the room and cleanses the warmth in the air.

"You forgot how to read?"

"I'm here to say I'm sorry about the fish. I didn't mean to let it go."

"You let it go?"

"No, but I thought I was holding it good enough."

"No, you were right the first time. I think you let it go."

I don't tell him that my father and Dox won't speak to me right now, too. They're still fuming.

"Why would I do that? I'm just as hungry as you."

"I doubt that."

I don't bite.

Fritter grimaces. "Guess that thing just wanted to live more than you wanted to eat it."

"I guess. But it doesn't have skin now."

"Who needs skin? It's swimming free."

"Don't tell me that."

Fritter puts his hand on the doorknob, but I push back against the door. If he wanted to, he could shut me out, no problem. He takes a step back. The door slowly swings open. I can see the wall where he last stopped.

Blisters have formed around the dents in the lid. Fritter slides the tip of the flathead into the coated groove of the paint can and lifts every few inches, going around in a full circle. I don't say anything. He frees the lid and begins to stir the paint with the screwdriver.

With the thinnest brush, he dabs the top skin and squats next to the spot on the wall. He picks up the spent bullet and holds it flush with where he left off.

"Plan on watching all day?" Fritter says.

"No."

"Okay."

"You planning on working all day?" I say.

"Depends."

"On what?"

"On if I have to hear that bike of yours tear out of here."

"I'm here now."

"He's been worried about you. He won't say it."

I almost answer Fritter. Instead, I point at the floor. "Why lines? Why not people or even animals?"

"You done?"

"I was just wondering."

"And I'm wondering why you don't get the fuck out of here." Fritter presses his meaty palm on the wall where it's wet. He doesn't turn around. He doesn't move at all.

"I'm leaving."

"Then leave already."

I LET FRITTER BE FRITTER and walk outside. It's so hot. All I want is to wash away the blue cat's blood that dried on my arms and chest. My father and Dox are sharing a bottle, jawing about how underappreciated fathers are. They are leaning up against the side wall of the boathouse that's looking like it will fall in at any moment. It's not for me to warn them.

I get on my dirt bike and start it up and crackle the air. No one asks me where I'm going. I lift my feet as I give it gas. The world wakes up just like the monster fish did, but this time I'm right on its tail, chasing it across the road and into the field. I smear a trail through the low clover. I can almost see the path all the way to the golf course and the enormous house and feel the AC that will greet my face and the warm water of the shower that will brush my skin.

I don't care what anyone thinks, not Mason or Wythe or any of the flies. I just want to be clean and have a chance to pretend. When I stare ahead, it's this fucking world that keeps coming at me. I have to squint to see it, and I want it to happen right now. I want to start, to finally grow up. And why can't it happen right this very second?

No amount of imagination will let me pretend myself into becoming a woman. I'm just a girl on a dirt bike in the middle of nowhere hauling ass and finding at that spot on the gas tank where it's flush with the seat that nothing is there, no blood at all.

I let off the gas and coast to a stop. The heat clings. My stomach is killing me. My body aches. If I could cut out the pain, it would be in the shape of the fish I would let go of, no question.

I call Mason and ask him what he's doing, and he tells me how a bunch of them are taking out Everett's father's boat and going waterskiing. I hold my breath. He doesn't ask me if I want to come with him.

"Will I see you later?" I say.

"Why?"

I tell myself, "Don't even think about it."

BACK WHEN WE LIVED NEAR the college, I would wait for the mail every day, but no cards or letters ever came. I began to think she had forgotten about me. My father said the program she had checked into wouldn't take long, and at first I believed him.

Junk mail was a different story. It seems no one told these companies that my mother was no longer here. We still received all of the catalogs she had signed up for. I gathered them into a pile and started cutting out the models that shared some trait with her. It might be the shape of the woman's hands or her mouth. Maybe even just the tilt of her neck.

I kept them all. I made a scrapbook with all of these parts. I never assembled them into one person. They just floated there, glued on construction paper. I was going to throw them all away the moment my mother came back to us.

It was during this same time that I started reading Anne Frank's diary, something my father had checked out for me from the children's literature section in the college library. Of course, I started keeping a diary myself, which was my father's hope all along, I suspect. He wanted me to write down my feelings, but I couldn't do it. And I wasn't interested in boys like Anne was so my entries were more just random thoughts, mostly nonsense. It was the nonsense that scared me the most.

The closest I ever came to knowing anything about boys back then was when I found some romance novels my mother had stashed among her things. There were scenes describing how men made women feel. The men had lots of muscles and grabbed at women and held them down. Everyone seemed to always be breathing heavily. Living, it seemed, was a chore. At one point I had to look up the word *flaccid*. Each time I read over certain scenes, I tried to imagine what these men were doing. I kept circling back to this one thought: I didn't want to be held down. I wondered if my mother had arrived at the same idea. I suspected she had.

Whenever I wrote, Marianne Moore would jump up on my bed and push herself against me. It was hard to concentrate with her licking my face and panting with her dog breath. My entries quickly turned to translations, or tried to. I was going to write what I thought Marianne Moore was thinking. That, however, didn't last long at all. I couldn't keep it up. I wasn't a real translator. The more I tried to think like Marianne Moore, to describe what crazy things she had already seen, the more I realized I was never going to be my mother.

IT WAS THE START OF a new school year, and my father began coming home from classes later and later. I was trying my hand at cooking, wanting to take the lessons my mother had already given me and to build on them. My father wouldn't eat the food I made for us on the stovetop. Instead, he mostly drank.

When he wasn't drinking, he was carrying lots of books in his leather satchel. The strap on the satchel eventually broke. He wrapped the strap with duct tape and even that separated. He carried home books in both arms. The sleeves of his suit coat began to rip, but he wasn't deterred. He brought home more books. He mumbled in French, as if I could understand him. My mother, at least, used to wait for us to go to sleep and then would read aloud the poems she was studying.

My father began to read the same poems aloud day and night.

Sometimes I thought my mother was in the other room.

My father stopped wearing suit coats and matching ties altogether, but he kept wearing vests. I washed his dress shirts, but they began to rip as well. I wanted to sew them, but there was no one to teach me how to sew. I tried on my own, but my sewing was crooked. When I asked him if he knew how to sew, if maybe he could teach me, he'd pat at a growing stack of student papers like they were Marianne Moore's head.

He didn't tell me my mother had been released months earlier. I think he was trying to protect me, though I had already seen the letter from the facility. More medical bills came to the house, too. I left them untouched. Packets from a law office would arrive, and I just did what my father asked. I stacked them in piles and left them unopened next to the growing stack of catalogs.

At night, he would read aloud from his pile of overdue library books. He was excited when he discovered a sheaf of onionskin pages my mother had typed up, was frantic when he found the corresponding handwritten notes. For the longest time, he thought she might actually come back for the work she had done. He gave up his own research and began to compile more for hers.

Those times when he passed out, I studied my mother's handwriting. The loops made me think of sitting on a pier. I was my mother as a girl watching the sky. As for my father, I didn't know what he was thinking. Some nights I would sit in my room and listen to my mother's words in his mouth. I told myself I wasn't going to fall apart. I was just going to turn something off inside me. Marianne Moore licked my face. I translated her gesture into "Everything is going to be fine, Pearl." But I couldn't write it down because that would have been a lie.

Mason and I don't talk for a week, and that's fine by me. Dox and my father took out Dox's boat and dragged a net in hopes of catching some puppy drum. Dox was upset to have used the gas with nothing to show for it, and so he went into town, busked for a few hours, and made enough to buy them another bottle.

My father acts different around me now, like I've done something terrible to myself. At night Dox seems stuck on playing "Drown," and I sit by the open window and listen to the slide.

I try to see the river out there and can do it if the moon lets me, if there aren't clouds. Fritter is slowly spinning in his room. I picture him floating in a river of his own making. I try not to think about the monstrous fish swimming in the dark, and how, if it's alive, it shouldn't be.

My father goes off walking. He takes Marianne Moore with him when he does, but they come back eventually, both intact. I tell myself as long as this lasts, this isn't such a bad life. Tomorrow I'll go to Mason's and pretend like nothing's happened, like everything's copacetic.

We lie in bed. The sheets smell like chemicals. They are meant to smell like flowers.

"You don't understand," Mason says.

"What don't I understand?"

"They want to erase us."

"Erase us?"

"Like we never existed."

"Okay," I say. "Hey, are you hungry?"

"That's it? I tell you there are people who want you gone, wiped off the face of the earth, and all you can say is 'Okay'?"

"Fine, let's get a little more precise here," I say. "Who is this *us* you're talking about?"

"You and me. Duh."

"So they want to make it so it's like you and I never existed?"

"Yeah."

"I'm not seeing that as such a bad thing."

"Yeah, right," he says. "Wait, are you being serious?"

THIS TIME IT'S REESE THAT grabs the assault rifle and steps up to the line marked in the field. He says it would be cool if his father used this at the next reenactment. "Can you even imagine?" Reese starts whistling "Dixie."

Fifty or so paces from us, the flies had put random stools and small tables in a row. If I squint, it looks like someone made a living room in the middle of nowhere.

Mason hands me a wooden crate filled with old vases and empty soda-pop bottles. "Do me a favor and go set these up out there."

Reese promises he won't hit me.

I expect Wythe to laugh the loudest, but he just eyes my legs, like he's trying to draw a bead on them.

I place the crate on the ground and reach for the vases first. Some of them are already chipped, but most are whole. I line them up. There are buttercups next to the crate. I pull some and drop a few in each vase. I do the same with the bottles.

When I turn around to head back, the flies are standing shoulder to shoulder, their arms crossed in front of their chests.

The only one that isn't is Reese, and that's because he's aiming the rifle right at me.

I stand next to Mason.

"Took you long enough," Wythe says. "Playing house?"

"Leave her alone," Mason says, and I can't believe it.

But the moment doesn't last. Reese lets loose and sprays my good work. I watch how something is clearly there one minute and isn't the next. The wood shatters with the glass. Never mind the flowers.

"That was fucked," Wythe yells.

The flies find their voices and chortle.

When they've had enough, Everett talks about taking out his father's boat again. They'll get some beers and sandwiches. They'll find an area that shallows and have some others meet them out there, where they'll tie the boats together and make a big floating mess of a party.

"Does that sound like fun?" Wythe says to me.

"I guess so."

He laughs. I already know I'm not invited.

WE TAKE ON WATER. I start scooping with coffee cans and shorn gallon milk jugs, scraping the bottom of Dox's boat. I wish my father and I had never taken it out. I fill and pour, fill and pour. Water keeps coming in a steady stream, though. I follow it back to where my father is leaning on the stern and one of the joints just below the clamped-on Evinrude buckles. As if it were waiting for me to witness the fracturing, it splits, and this seam of the river pushes inward and begins to weigh us down further.

"Can we make it?" I stare at the shore.

My father shakes his head. He frowns. The boards of the stern finally give way, and the motor drops, submerges fully. The plugs are wet now and useless. Above it hovers a quick, bitter cloud of smoke.

One thing my mother once said was to never leave a boat. It was her uncle's advice from when she was a girl. You can turn the boat so that it's hull side up. That makes it easier to spot. My father tries to loosen the motor's clamp. He's dunking for apples, but the boat doesn't care. It keeps dropping. It wouldn't matter anyway. We're not rich enough for the coast guard to come looking for us.

. . .

The river wants to reach us and keeps filling the boat. We're waist high in rising water. The coffee cans float and the milk jugs float upright, but the net, bunched like fabric, goes down. The rest of the boat goes down after it.

I manage to hold on to one of the oars and set the stringer of croaker on top of it. My father surfaces in a rush of bubbles. His nostrils flare, and he takes half of the sky inside him.

"No use," he says.

"Is it gone?"

"It's gone."

I don't know which way is closest to the shore, but my father starts bobbing up and down, spinning slowly in a circle. He squints and covers his eyes each time he reaches his highest point.

"I can see the bridge," he says.

My heart sinks. I remember the bridge. I thought we were closer to the inlet.

"It's okay," I say. "We'll make it."

"I hate that bridge."

"I hate it, too."

We leave it at that.

I LET HIM LEAD THE WAY, but soon I'm kicking alongside him. I keep looking from side to side, scanning the water.

"What are you looking for, Pearl?"

"I don't want to say."

"Probably better that way."

"Yeah."

We keep a steady pace until I stop.

"Cramp?" he says.

"Let's just float here for a second."

I grab the back of my right leg and knead my hamstring.

"Come here," he says. "Here."

My father pulls me to him. I put my arm over his chest. He's going to carry me. I want to cry because I can feel the deep breaths as he holds them. We float toward the shore. I try to keep all images of bull sharks out of my mind. They're the kind that can move between salt water and freshwater. They have it in them to live anywhere. Maybe that could be my favorite animal.

By the time we reach to where we can stand, it is early evening. The sky has started to dim. There are so many trees it's hard to tell where we are, but my father looks around and then I see his horse teeth.

"Might want to throw them back." He points at the croaker. "If any are still alive."

"How are your legs?"

"Pins and needles, but it's going away."

"What do we tell Dox about the boat?"

"The truth," my father says. "That it was a beautiful piece of shit."

"He'll say it was working when we left."

"Let him put it in a song. I don't care."

AFTER MASON FINISHES, we lie in bed. I close my eyes. My heart is still going. Out of the blue, he asks me if I'll be starting school this fall. I grunt, but he doesn't laugh. He says, "Wythe thinks we should use the field for a party next month, bring out a generator and invite some bands, but I don't know."

"What field?"

"You know what field. Our field."

"I didn't know we had a field."

"Well, we do."

"That's sweet."

"It's not sweet."

I turn over. I rest my hands and chin on his chest. His hair splays across the pillow and disappears against the white cotton pillowcase. If I blink, his body will fuse with the bed.

"I was just thinking," I say. "It could be our first official date."

Mason snorts. "Hardly."

"You can be that way, but it could."

"You mean it could be if I asked you."

"Then ask me."

"I'm not asking you."

"What about when school starts back up? Won't there be some kind of homecoming dance? I imagine there are lots of dances."

"Listen to you."

"Well, aren't there?"

"Yeah, you dress up. It's all pretty stupid."

"That doesn't sound stupid to me."

"God, don't become a girl."

"What?"

"Now you want to dress up and hang out. I didn't think you liked my friends."

"I don't like them, but I don't hate them. Plus, I wouldn't be hanging out with them. Not really."

"I don't see how."

"I would be with you. And by the way, I am a girl, so fuck off."

"*Tranquila, mi corazón. Tranquila.*"

I put weight on his breastbone just to do it. His chest still rises and sinks.

"Last I checked you didn't own a dress." He smirks.

"I own a dress."

His expression doesn't change. "You don't."

"You could buy me one."

"I'm not buying you a dress."

"I could make one then."

"Good one, Cinderella."

"If I make one, would you take me?"

"Are you even listening to yourself?" The lenses of his Way-farers are black paint. "Here, get up for a second. I can't breathe. It's hard to breathe when you're on me like this."

I move off him. He stands up on the bed and stares down at me. There's so much white hair under and around his crotch. It looks like he sat on a clump of corn silk. He steps off the mattress and walks over to one of the cameras. He adjusts the lens and then hits a button and the corner glows red. I pull the end of the sheet up to my neck and keep my fists bunched.

"I tell you what," Mason says, off-camera. "Why don't you do this. Why don't you make an argument for why I should take you as a date. But you have to give it to me. I mean, really give it to me, okay?"

"Fine."

"I'm ready when you are."

I DON'T FEEL LIKE I should have to answer the question, but I do. I start telling him as he stands there behind the camera. I talk about how my father and I live and how we don't have much. I watch him get hard as I talk. He looks down suddenly, as if unaware of his body. He spits in his hand and rubs it all over.

I tell him about the blue cat I caught and skinned, and how it fought out of my grasp to vanish into the river. I keep talking, telling him how slippery it was. I start pleading my case even more. I tell him I love it here, in this very room. That he lets me clean myself in the shower, that he feeds me, that he's so, so big, even though he isn't. That's when he closes his eyes.

I go on and tell him what makes me so special. I'm a word in a poem. I'm a thing my parents fought over more than once, just to get it right. *Precision, Pearl.* But he isn't paying attention anymore. I'm just watching him. I don't even know what I've been saying. When he comes, he almost hits himself under the chin. We laugh, and that's when I get out bed and walk over to where he collapses on the floor. I wipe at his neck with my fingers, and I take those same fingers and pull them apart slowly, studying the viscous fluid, its stickiness. The slime is so much like the coating of the blue cat that I can't stop rubbing it.

"Eat it," he whispers.

"You eat it."

He pulls away from me.

"What?" I say.

"You're fucked-up. I'm not eating it."

"Why should I have to be the one to eat it?"

"Because that's what you're supposed to do. You love it."

"I do?"

"That's right."

I stare up at the skylights. They glow above us.

"I'm not sure I love it," I say.

"All women love it."

"I'm not sure all women love it."

I want him to stop talking, but he can't help himself.

"If you're a real woman," he says, laughing, "then you'd love it."

"I'm calling bullshit on that."

I have to cup my hand now, to keep it all there.

"You've seen the same videos as me," he says.

It all comes back to what we've seen.

"Those were lies," I say.

The camera is recording an empty bed.

I lean over to him like I'm going to kiss him and, instead, wipe my hand on his chest.

"What the fuck was that for?" Mason says.

"It belongs to you. I'm just giving it back."

"I didn't want it back."

I laugh now. "You should taste it at least."

"Why do you keep saying that?"

"Don't you want to know what you taste like?"

"Why are you acting like this, Pearl?"

"Like what?"

"I don't know. All crazy."

He wants us to take a shower together, but I won't now. I climb back into bed and cover myself with the sheet. I hide my face.

"Turn off the camera," I say.

"I will after we fuck." He leaves the camera on as he walks into the bathroom. I hear the water start up.

He's no longer Mason. He's Main Boy. That's who he's always been.

I get dressed.

While Main Boy's still in the shower, I sneak into his father's study. I take down the fly rod and grab the creel and a pack of flies. I leave the house and sprint to where I've stashed my dirt bike in the woods.

"Fuck the dance," I keep singing in my head.

The dirt bike sings back.

WHEN I GET HOME, FRITTER is waiting for me on the back porch. The pickup is off to the side of the boathouse, idling near the gutted washing machines.

"Where've you been?" Fritter stares at the fly rod.

"Nowhere."

"That's a long time to be nowhere."

"What's wrong?"

"Get in the truck, and I'll tell you on the way."

"It's Marianne Moore, isn't it? I knew it."

We climb in the cab. I put the things on the floorboard.

"It's not about her," Fritter says as we reverse to a stop. He shifts it into gear and punches the gas. "It's your father."

We fly down the road.

"Is he okay?"

"We don't know yet. He's not talking."

"*Not* talking?"

"He can't even make a sentence."

FRITTER SAYS DOX WAS THE one who saw him fall. Earlier, in the afternoon, my father was playing like he was going to dive off the pier again. He took a swig from his bottle and then went to the edge, bending his knees and fake bouncing like he was ready to launch out over the water. But Dox says something was off in my father's face. He spins around and gives Dox this look like he doesn't know where he is, like his face was hit head-on by a sadness, and his knees buckle and his eyes roll back, and though Dox calls for him, my father doesn't look up, because he's already collapsing into the air just above the river and then into the river itself.

In my mind, I can see it unfolding. Dox grows stronger right there and shoots across the yard, diving headfirst into the water, and though Dox is a small man, he grabs my father around the chest and puts him on his hip as he does a sidestroke back to the muddy bank. Fritter comes out of the house just as my father is having a seizure.

Dox says, "Don't touch him, son, let him finish," and the two stand off to the side watching my father convulse while Dox coughs up water at the same time. Once my father's body has stopped shaking, Dox checks his pulse and also his breathing. Though my father seems stable, he won't wake up now. Dox starts crying and asks where I am. No one knows because I haven't told them. Dox says, "Leave her a note so she's not scared when she comes back and finds us gone," and Fritter says he runs back inside, the adrenaline saving his bad ankles for the time being, and looks around and decides to paint a quick message in the white space above his mural—*Don't worry, we're okay*—then he runs out and lifts my father into the truck bed. They push aside some things to make room. Dox climbs in and cradles my father's head. The three of them take off, driving this same route we're on, miles and miles from the nearest hospital.

The truck shudders. I look over at the speedometer. We're going almost ninety. It doesn't matter. There are no speed-limit signs on this stretch. They've all been blown off their posts.

"HOW FAR NOW?" I ASK.

The river is on our left, chasing alongside us.

"Twenty klicks," Fritter says.

"What's that mean?"

"What it means."

The truck's shuddering makes my shins rub against the creel.

"Maybe we should go slower," I say.

"Don't you want to get there?"

"Alive, yes."

"We're fine. We're alive now."

The truck shakes harder. It feels like one of the wheels is going to roll off.

"I don't think we're fine. Just for the record."

"Going fishing?" he says, trying to distract me.

"Yeah."

"Where did you get it?"

"Where I got it."

I look right at him. Two can play this game.

We start slowing down.

I sigh. "Thanks. I was worried—"

"Why are you thanking me?" He is stomping the gas pedal, but the truck keeps slowing.

We coast to a stop.

FRITTER TRIES TO START IT a bunch of times, but it won't turn over. The electrical is shot. No lights on the dashboard come on.

"Alternator," he says.

"No battery?"

"That's right."

"My phone is dead, too. I should've been charging it this whole time."

"Dead just like this mother—"

Fritter pounds the steering wheel.

Before we abandon the truck, we take a quick inventory of what we have. The double barrel that was behind the bench seat is back at the boathouse. There are no shells for it anyway. What is stashed in its place is a canvas tool bag with some tie wraps, a small knife, and a rusty handsaw. I pick up the creel with the fly rod, and Fritter carries everything else. We don't stay on the road, but cross over the embankment to follow the river.

I can still see the truck when a breath catches in my throat.

"We left Marianne Moore," I say.

"Fuck."

"She can take care of herself, right?"

"If she can't, we'll find out."

At our pace, we're a solid day's walk from Dox and my father. That is, if Fritter's ankles hold. I can't tell if he's laughing or crying now. We can't head back to the road and hitch a ride because we're who we are. I know that much. Fritter says we can walk on the loam and that might help some, so there's that.

Up ahead is more field and more rows of Silver Queen corn and, of course, more and more river. The river is endless.

We follow it, and I can see the current trotting alongside us like Marianne Moore. What I wouldn't give for one of those faint skiffs in the distance to come forward and pull up alongside us. I would even take a ride from one of Main Boy's friends, a speedboat loaded with partyers while Fritter and I were dragged behind it on one of those huge inner tubes.

"Watch it." Fritter holds up a fist.

I stop marching and suck in my breath. I crouch like him and get low.

A white pickup tears down a dirt road up ahead, pulls dust behind it like a parachute.

"What's this motherfucker want?" Fritter growls, but the white truck is a toy now, it's that far away. The blur of it has gone from our sight and disappeared into a glob of sycamores that cover a point up ahead.

"Should we wait here or what?" I say.

"I have to sit anyway."

I scan the branches. Water moccasins are hanging off like tied-together pairs of shoes thrown over phone lines. When I set the creel down, Fritter asks me if he can take a peek. I hand everything over to him, and he's gentle with each piece. He tells me the joining ends are called *ferrules*, and I nod like that's a given.

"This is pretty nice stuff. You know how to use one of these?"

"It was a gift."

"Okay, but do you know how to use one?"

"I was planning to teach myself."

He smiles at me like he knows something I don't.

"When I was your age, all I did was fly-fish. But not a nice one like this here."

I try not to show my surprise.

"You don't believe me?"

"Just seems funny, that's all."

"What? What's funny?"

"I'm not going to say it."

"I wasn't bad."

I pause. "You think he's going to be okay?"

"Now, don't do that."

"What?"

"Stay positive. He's in a better place. Besides, Dox is there with him."

"A better place," I say, repeating the phrase.

"That's right."

"That's what people say when someone dies."

"I didn't mean he was dead."

"Okay."

"Here, you want a quick casting lesson?"

"I'll take a rain check."

THE WHITE TRUCK COMES BACK the way it came, down the path and pulling its parachute. For a moment, I think it's Main Boy's father, but there's no way. I don't want it to be him.

When the white truck gets to the paved road, it turns left, cutting the parachute loose. It heads in the same direction we need to go.

"Come on," Fritter says, but I have to help him up.

"Your ankles."

He hobbles like he's barefoot and the ground is shards.

By the time we reach the bend, Fritter has to rest again, but I push on him when I see a clearing in the trees near the point. In the clearing is a cinder-block foundation and some framed walls going up on top of it. Next to it is a stack of wood, with the legs of sawhorses poking out from a huge gray tarp.

"Building me a house?" I say.

"That's right. A beautiful mansion."

"With my own room?"

"Of course."

"And my own bathroom with a claw-foot tub and a sink and a big mirror that reflects everything."

"You've been thinking a lot about this, huh?"

"It's how I like to fall asleep."

"That's good."

"What's good?"

"To still have dreams."

"I still have dreams."

"If you say so."

"Don't say that."

We beeline it over to the tarp and pull it back. There are power tools—saws, a compressor, and a nail gun—and a refrigerator-size generator next to beige army-grade containers. Some of the containers are empty, and others are still filled with gasoline. Stacked behind the generator are ropes and electrical cords placed one on top of the other.

"White Truck done us a solid," Fritter says, and wants me to fist bump. I hold up a fist. He hits mine and pretends that his hand is a grenade that explodes right between us.

"This is a lot of shit," I say.

"Yes, it is. So?"

"So?" I'm smiling now.

"So get to it."

"Get to what?"

He shakes his dreadlocks. If they were beaded, they would be one of those hippie curtain doors. "Everything we need is here."

"Okay," I say, though I don't know where he's going with this.

He points at the river and then at the half-finished frame. "Is it just me or does that wall already look like a raft?"

"WHAT IF WHITE TRUCK COMES BACK?" I say.

"Fuck White Truck."

"I know, but what if it does?"

"Pearl."

"Yeah?"

"Do you want to get there or not?"

"Of course I do."

"Then shut the fuck up, please."

Fritter digs through the tools and finds sledgehammers and a couple of crowbars. He hands me one of each and starts busting the corner of a wall loose. I try to get at the other end but nothing budges.

"Scoot over," he says. "If we had more time, I'd show you what I'm doing."

"Fine."

He swings the hammer and things break. He loosens this other end and then pushes right in the middle. We have to jump back before it crashes down. The skeletal frame that's left just leans.

"It's not pretty." He taps the makeshift raft. "But it should work. Especially if we put some of those canisters under it."

We bust away the extra two-by-fours that had splintered off at the ends. We try to pull it over to the bank of the river. It's a chore because Fritter's feet are killing him. We wedge the empty canisters in any spot of the frame that will allow them to fit. We turn the whole thing over so it's sheet side up.

"You think it'll float?" I say.

"The river will let us know quick if it won't."

WE AIM THE RAFT TOWARD deeper water. Fritter pushes down too much on one side, and the raft nearly sinks. He sprawls across the deck like he's been shot. The raft makes like it's going to keep dropping down, but then it does something amazing: it springs back and levels out.

"Look at this," Fritter says.

"What am I looking at?"

Fritter gets on all fours and then eases himself to standing. He grins and puts his hands on his hips like he's king of the mountain. "Perfection."

"Don't forget, it needs to hold me, too."

"Shoot, you're barely there."

Fritter tells me to grab some two-by-fours, and I hand them to him. I also give him the fly rod and the creel, and our canvas bag filled with our own tools. The tarp I grab just to take it.

"I feel like we should leave a thank-you note," I say, still standing in the water.

"Girl, get your ass on this raft."

. . .

We push on the soft bottom of the river. We find where the run weaves like cordage with other currents and gains speed. We catch on a part of the conveyor belt with our displacement. The landscape starts to slide past.

"You get to steer," Fritter says.

"Really?"

I grab one of the two-by-fours. I try to touch the bottom, but I can't. I even push the upper end of the two-by-four just under the surface of the water. We're gliding along in a spot where the river is too deep.

"There's no steering this raft, is there?" I say.

Fritter laughs.

WE DRIFT INTO THE EVENING. The river gets to look like it's a sliver of glass. I'm starving, but I don't say it. It's a given.

I wonder if they're feeding my father.

Fritter stands in the middle of the raft and doesn't say anything. He's assembled the rod and is tying a fly pattern on the end of the leader.

"You think it's still out there?" Fritter says.

"Is what still out there?"

"Your fish."

I look at him.

"What?" he says.

He shakes his head.

His head is on fire.

Fritter pulls out so much excess floating line from the reel that it bunches near his feet. He flicks some of the line forward and then puts his head down, like he's saying a prayer.

"You okay there?" I say.

He nods and lifts his head. When he does, he also brings his right forearm back quickly. He stops his hand by his ear, like he's listening to a seashell. The squiggle of line that had been floating on the river flings back behind him. Unlike my father, he doesn't talk me through what he's doing.

I study it all, every detail. He slides his arm forward to a sudden stop. His dreadlocks don't move. The rod, curved like a bow, pulls the line hanging in the air behind him. All of the stored energy forms a tight loop that unrolls to a finite point on the air. I catch my breath.

Before the floating line can drift down onto the water's surface, he repeats the action with the back cast. The whole thing is so elegant.

"I had no idea," I say.

He doesn't look at me.

"Has it been a long time?"

"Yeah, but it comes back to you. This is called false casting."

Fritter grins, and something about his face softens. For the first time, I feel like I glimpse what he must have looked like when he was younger, when he was a boy. After a few more casts, he holds out the fly rod to me, but I shake my head.

"How many tours did you do?"

He goes back to casting, the line rolling and unrolling above him. "Don't ask me that."

The river keeps sliding on either side of us.

"Do you ever miss it?" I say.

"Each time I left, I hated being gone."

"That seems like the opposite."

"It doesn't make sense, does it?"

"No."

"I think you get used to living a certain way."

"Do you ever want to go back?" I say.

He slaps his gut and smiles. "They wouldn't take me back."

"How do you know? Have you tried?"

"I just know *I* wouldn't even take me back."

"HOW LONG UNTIL WE GET THERE, do you think?"

"Tomorrow sometime."

"That seems too long."

"The current's moving pretty quick, so maybe sooner."

"So what you're saying is that we're at the mercy of the river."

"When haven't we been at the mercy of this river?" Fritter says.

We keep drifting.

"Are you happy?" I say.

"Am I *what*?"

"Happy."

"Why would you ask me something like that?"

"It's a harmless question."

"If you say so."

"You keep saying that. You think it isn't?"

"I think it's rude."

"You think it's rude to ask someone if they're happy?"

"I do."

I look at my hands.

"What about you?" Fritter says.

"Me?"

"Yeah."

"You're asking me if I'm happy?"

"I am."

I don't answer.

"See, it's a silly question, isn't it?"

The river vanishes. It's just Fritter talking, but I stop listening. All I can think about is my father. I should've complained more about his drinking. I should've made it a point to check his feet more than I did. I feel like I've failed him.

"It's not freezing," Fritter says, when I finally tune in. "But it's damn near close to it. I was young the first time I fished the shad run."

I have to stop him now. "What's the shad run?"

"It's when the fish migrate from the ocean and return to the river to spawn."

"Isn't there a word for that?"

"*Anadromous*," Fritter says, without skipping a beat. "Dox had left us that spring. He didn't take any of his things with him. He came back, but not until later. I was tiny then, too."

"I'm trying to picture a tiny Fritter," I say, but he doesn't laugh.

"I wanted to fish the run so badly I put on three pairs of Dox's pants, bundled up, and waded in the cold water. No one was around to tell me I was doing something wrong."

He goes on to explain how he just cast straight across and would let his line dead drift. When it finally swung near the bank, that's when he felt the knocks on the line, like there was this door floating under the river.

"The first time I pulled up, I was answering those knocks. Like Dox had come back to my mom and me already. I hooked into one. It was all loose voltage. When I pulled on the line, I could feel the fish on the other end."

I close my eyes and listen to him go on. I can see this first fish leaping in the air, how it would leap three more times. I could see everything perfectly. Light turned the scales a silvered blue and lavender. When I open my eyes, Fritter is smiling.

"Funny how this one memory has stayed with me. Probably more so than any other. You asked me if I was happy? This was probably the happiest I had ever been in my life, Pearl."

Thick fog appears on the river. I think we should start trying for the nearest shore, settle in until it passes, but Fritter says to stay the course. It sounds like something my father would say.

Fritter's dreadlocks bunch under his head like a pillow made from piled skeins of yarns. His eyes start closing, and soon he's asleep with his mouth open. His face goes soft again. I can see the boy in him, long before he grew up and put on a uniform to measure the world through a rifle's scope.

THE FOG FINDS EVERY SPACE that isn't us. Fritter lies on the raft and snores lightly. I grin. Deep down I've always loved a good joke. Main Boy's not the only one. Dox says there's no way to get through life without laughing as much as possible. Maybe I should blame Dox for what I do next, because a voice in my head tells me I should pretend we're back home, that the raft has carried us in reverse, that we're actually safe.

I start a conversation with my father and tell him about White Truck and the wall we made into a raft, and the empty canisters we used underneath for floatation, and when Fritter stirs, I say, "Dox, remember that fish I caught and we skinned it, but it came back to life, Dox, wasn't that unbelievable? And it swam away, Dox, it did. Without its skin, Dox." I even start clapping.

Fritter sits up and rubs his eyes. His face is still soft with sleep. He's that boy wanting to tell someone about the dream he just had. The fog is all around us, and I just keep talking to Dox. I go on about the blue cat swimming in the dark. In my mind I'm thinking how that fish has also vanished into the darkness Fritter won't stop painting, and I say, "Dox, that would make a good song, wouldn't it?" Fritter, stunned now, says, "Dox, is that you?" His eyes pop open. Before I can stop him, he makes like he's about to roll out of bed. The raft dips down on his end, and like that, Fritter slides into the blur of the river and is gone.

SOME OF THE FOG GOES into the water with him. The river gulps it down. I freeze. I keep saying Fritter's name under my breath, as if that will help, but it doesn't help.

Fritter surfaces like a submarine spearing a sheet of ice. He gasps. He keeps screaming my name like he's lost me, me his entire life. I'm his daughter now and he's my father, but away from, farther from the idea of who he is. My father is no longer in the hospital connected to machines because he, like my mother, doesn't exist anymore.

He throws his chest onto the raft, and the raft lifts like a drawbridge. I almost roll off. Fritter squirms back on. The raft crashes down and levels out. Fritter breathes heavily, shivering each time he exhales.

"Sorry. It was meant to be a joke. I didn't think you were going to go in the water."

"Yeah."

"We should get over to the bank. I'll start us a fire."

He doesn't answer.

He holds his chest. We drift.

"Fritter?"

"Yeah."

"You mad at me?"

"No, I'm not mad."

"Angry?"

"That's the same thing."

"It's not."

"I'm not mad or angry."

"Disappointed?" It's what my father would say.

"Not disappointed at all," Fritter says.

"What then?"

"Nothing. I'm nothing."

I TAKE THE TARP AND roll an end around one of the two-by-fours, like I'm rolling up part of a flag. I pull the knife out of the canvas tool bag and make three-inch cuts near the hem of the opposite end of the tarp. If I were writing in my journal, my father would call these marks *virgules*, those grammatical slashes placed between words for meaning "either this or that." Or both, fusing like a stitch. Whenever I see a virgule wedged between two words, I think of it as being between two *worlds*, separating one side from the other.

The river is a virgule.

Fritter doesn't ask me what I'm doing. He just watches and waits. I take another two-by-four. I weave it over and under all the quick cuts I've made with the knife, until this second two-by-four is threaded nearly half the length of the tarp. Now we have a rudder. Fritter still hasn't said a word. He shivers.

AT FIRST, THERE IS THE wheeze of brush and then the percussive snaps of the driest branches. The fire builds in increments. It goes from grass to twigs to branches to a scooped half of a fallen trunk the size of a human head. I pull more chunks apart like bread. I've made a larger fire than I'd intended, but Fritter doesn't complain.

His shirt is off and he holds his hands palms out, and the fire rounds and domes like a massive snow globe. I think this could be a nice moment if we weren't heading where we were heading, and if I hadn't felt the need to play a trick. Maybe I've been around the flies too long.

Fritter isn't shivering anymore, his shirt hanging in a nearby tree. Though I've seen him shirtless before, all the generous folds of him on display, the shadows cast by the fire do something to his body. Maybe it's where I'm sitting now. On his left side, just under his arm, I see for the first time are peppered clumps of scar tissue. They're braided pink and gray in the flickering light. It looks like he slept on a shell collection.

I DREAM ABOUT THE FLIES. If there's a line of trees in my dream, the trees will shatter into a trillion punctuation marks and form again. They become part of the land that Fritter and I walk. They swirl underfoot to a bridge spanning a body of water rushing underneath. Fritter and I stand near the edge, and the flies, the shadows broken off into boys, goad one of them to slip a thin line around his ankles and climb onto the railing to launch out and plunge downward, the entire descent his skin shivering into bits of flies, until the bungee cord stretches taut and the boy springs back up and over, his friends stomping and punching one another, their idiocy palpable as they wait with grabby hands for him to drift safely into their collective grasp.

Fritter and I just watch, but soon the same boy and the line flatten out, fusing, and stretch into one long cord that coils around Fritter's ankles, and he, without so much as a sigh, says, "I guess I'm next," and he hops onto the railing. I'm suddenly mad, telling him to get back down this instant, but he just shrugs, like he doesn't have a choice, and when I finally scream, nothing comes out and it's that silence that tips him over, I know it, and Fritter plunges downward, his massive body hurtling as the line of flies stretches until it's pulled taut, a popping sound, but Fritter doesn't stop—instead the soles of his feet are attached to the dangling line, but the rest of his body continues to fall with increasing velocity.

And why can't I imagine jet fire pouring out of the ends of each amputation, that the ends of his ankles are suddenly the exhaust of rocket engines, instead of blood that whisks into flies? Everything about him vanishes and breaks apart before impact, like a satellite finding its way back to earth, except there's no satellite, it's a body made of flies, and there's no river below because there's no earth to hold it in place, what was once earth vanishes at impact, and—*Poof! Ta-da!*—everything is flies.

WHEN I OPEN MY EYES, the fog has lifted. It's getting light out. The fire has grown smaller. Fritter yanks his shirt down from the branches and puts it back on.

"How long was I gone?" I say.

"I don't know. I wasn't watching you."

"I want to get there right now."

"We will. We're not far from the bridge. When we see it, we'll know we're there."

"I feel like I was gone a long time."

"Funny how that is."

"Did you feed it?" I point at the fire with my chin.

"I fed it."

The fire warbles above the embers.

I grab the fly rod from the raft and wade out into the river. Fritter stands on the shore and watches me. I try to remember what he did, how he was able to make the line move smoothly from one point in front of him to one point behind him. I move the line around, but the fly swings back and catches on the front of my shorts. I yell, laughing at the same time. I unhook myself and throw the line on the water.

"That was embarrassing," I say.

"No, you did good. Just next time, catch a fish."

Fritter stands across from me like he's my mirror image. His left foot is forward and his right foot is back, and he's holding his right arm off to the side and cocked at an angle above his waist. I get the line out in front of me and hold my right arm in the same way and with my left hand hold the excess line closest to the reel, the reel that is still as bright as I remember it from the first time I saw it in Main Boy's father's study. Fritter sees me look up again, and he nods as if to start, and like that, in sync, we sway.

I mimic the way he pulls his arm back and stops, watching the line spring from the river and unroll out behind me. He moves forward, I move forward. He moves back, I move back. Our false casts perfectly timed like some Olympic event, and here's the sad part, if it can even be called such a thing: never before have I felt more connected to anyone in my life. Not to my father or mother, not even during the times I spent in Main Boy's bed wrapped in cool sheets, or with him in his shower, when he was forcing himself inside me, when he was saying, "You fucking love this, don't you?" and it couldn't be the furthest thing from the truth.

But with Fritter guiding me, and my hands his hands and my arms his arms, if he were to ask me this same question, in even the same grunting way that Main Boy had, I would scream, "Yes, I love this, I do!"

Is it pathetic that I start to cry?

"Stop it," Fritter says, and drops his arms. "He'll be fine. You'll see."

I reel in the line. The sun burns away the rest of the mist. We can see the breadth of the river and even a nearby field of more Silver Queen. I look over at Fritter. His body is layers of other bodies, other versions of himself. His dreadlocks are frozen paths of fire-works. His head is torn cordage that's unraveled. I can't stop my-self from wanting him to be something more. I keep reeling in the line that has dipped under the surface. For a moment, it seems hooked to Fritter and pulls with it even the field behind him.

"YOU HUNGRY?"

That's always the question.

"I could eat," I say.

That's always the answer.

We both laugh.

Fritter says his ankles feel a little better. We leave the embers going and walk into the corn. He points forward, stabbing to where the silk glistens from first light. I can't help thinking of Main Boy again.

I think we're going to pull down as many ears of corn as we can carry, but Fritter keeps going. He pushes through the tall stalks. We slip deeper into the field. At one point, I stop and break off an ear and strip it back to look at the white corn. It's rows of baby teeth.

"Too young," I say, but Fritter keeps going. "Hey, did you hear me?"

"I heard you." He slows his pace.

The stalks close in behind me.

He holds up a fist. I stop and stand still.

The sun warms us even more.

• • •

Fritter starts singing quietly. We could be back at the boathouse, goofing with Dox on his cigar-box guitar while my father sits on the pier and slaps his leg on the offbeat. Just then, Fritter punches into the corn. His fist disappears. When he pulls back his arm, he's holding up a snake.

It forms a wriggling coil around his arm. It burns bright and alive. Fritter squeezes below its jaws. The snake opens its mouth. It's going to give us a piece of its mind.

FRITTER COULD BE OPENING a bottle of orange Crush. He pops off the head. The snake doesn't care that its head is gone. Its body, fizzing, keeps moving in the coil it created along his arm. I can feel its energy charging the air between us.

Fritter turns it upside down and gives it a few jolts. He fishes his fingers into the wound he's made and finds the skin, clamping on to it. I can only think of my father now, his pulling the double barrel from its leather case. The image fuses with Fritter stripping the snake's muscular body from its skin. The skin is a crisp, wet sock he discards in the stalks.

We walk back to our little fire. The embers lay hidden under the ash. All it takes is a stirring from a branch. The glowing red insides do their best *ta-da*. I throw on more wood. Flames bring their teeth and nibble and spin around the branches like corn. Fritter drops wrapped ears right on them. On the unshucked leaves goes the snake, but then Fritter immediately reaches back into the fire and grabs the body.

"Look here." He squeezes an opening near the tail, and out pop three small globes chained together with goo. Fritter grins and calls them "pearls," but I know they're eggs. I get the knife and stab its blade a few times into the fire to cook off whatever is on the rust. Fritter dribbles the pearls onto the blade and they fry up in two shakes.

The eggs taste like a memory of eggs.

We wait for the meat to go opaque.

Not long ago we had lots of chickens. If I wanted breakfast, I would wake and creep through the stacks of pallets out back to peer into the open washing machines. I was searching for eggs, but the chickens never left them on the straw bedding of the coop where I could find them. Dox said all chickens were a nervous bunch.

They often got loose and dropped their eggs all over the yard. They hid them from us like it was a game. Eggs that weren't rotten I'd boil and pick them clean for the others, leaving them in a bowl next to a splash of salt packets. For mine, I'd take our sharpest knife and make the thinnest slices possible, the kind where you can almost see through the white of the egg, and once I was done, I'd set the knife down and eat a slice and wait, eat a slice and wait, until I my plate was empty.

Fritter bites into one of the ears of corn. "Tastes like snake."

I grin. We make short work of it all.

We scrape dirt over the embers. We're hiding the fire in the ground.

"We should get a move on," Fritter says, and I'm already freeing the two-by-fours from the tarp. We use them to push the raft back into the current. It's still early morning, but the sun doesn't know it yet. When we get into a wide-open section of the river, I have to shield my eyes it's so bright out.

• • •

We drift past newly built docks that meander through pampas grass and cattails. They settle near trim, bright green lawns looking shellacked with light. Downriver is the big bridge. When you're right up on it, it emerges from the water sleek and polished white, but from here, head-on, the bridge looks less alien, more like a giant piece of scrimshaw.

On one of the docks we pass are young boys, probably ten and younger. They're throwing rigs that spin like mobiles hanging over cribs. Dangling from the hooks are chunks of cut bait. Everywhere we look there is laughter.

The boys are trying to heave their rigs close to us. I don't have to squint to make out their thrilled faces. The rigs drop far away from where we are, some ten yards, if not more, but with each plunk the boys howl louder. Anyone would think they had hit us for sure.

"If we didn't have somewhere to be, I'd swim over there and teach those little bastards a lesson," Fritter growls.

NOT LONG AFTER WE CAME to live with Dox and Fritter, my father and I were walking the perimeter of the property. He wanted to get the lay of the land. I kept trying to picture my mother here. My father, on the other hand, wore a felt hat cocked low like some kind of gentleman farmer. He would lazily swing a branch he'd fashioned into a walking stick and launch into a sermon on what he called "the ecology of our recent situation." He didn't think I had seen him earlier, when he had happened upon a moldy encyclopedia stacked in one of the closets upstairs.

"Take a look at this, Pearl." My father bent to pick up the husk of an insect.

"What is it?"

"Belostomatidae."

"Do what?"

"That's its name."

"That's its name?"

"Well, actually, its family. Kingdom Animalia, phylum Arthropoda, class Insecta, order Hemiptera, family . . ."

"Belostomatidae."

"Correct."

"But why not just *toe-biter*?"

"Okay, toe-biter, yes. But which one is more precise?"

"I know I should say the first one."

"Yes?"

"But I'm going with the second one."

"Have it your way, Pearl."

Before we circled back, my father asked me if I knew the males were the ones that carried the eggs on their backs. He gestured to the journal I clutched like a purse. "Make sure you write that in there, that the males carry the eggs. You hear me?"

"I heard you. The males are these amazing caregivers. The males can do no wrong. Anything else I should know?"

"I think that covers it for now. Class dismissed."

IT TAKES US ALMOST ANOTHER hour of drifting to get to the bridge, and when we finally do, Fritter and I can only stare up at the trusses. Giant rivets and bolts hold together the intricate steelwork underneath. It's strange to be here with a view of something so enormous and rigid, to gaze behind the scenes of such a monstrosity.

Tents cover half of the park where my mother and I had once let Marianne Moore run free. Overhead, gulls spin. I'm hoping my eyes are deceiving me, but it's real. We've arrived at the start of a Civil War reenactment. The park is awash in a sea of wool uniforms and muskets. Some of the soldiers parade around Confederate flags. In between cheers, we hear bluegrass music.

Catty-cornered from the park is the hospital. Sunlight brushes some of the windows. I construct the makeshift rudder and get the raft to pull portside this time. I'm trying to hurry.

"What do you think they're celebrating?" I say.

"You don't want me to answer that."

. . .

Fritter takes off his shirt and slips into the river. Half-submerged, he suddenly looks weightless, floating behind the raft. He starts singing. His dreadlocks drown in the water, and his huge chest stretches smooth of any folds. His voice is sharp as a knife. I get in with him and let the water cover me up. We get the raft in a shallow stretch and drag it up onto the bank.

He grabs his shirt and I grab the fly rod, the creel, and the canvas tool bag. We're drenched and reek of the river. It's not long before we merge into a throng of grown men with muttonchops and other versions of unruly facial hair. They're dressed in dark blue wool uniforms. Some have shiny epaulets perched on their shoulders, their golden tentacles sprawling.

Other soldiers start checking their phones. We march alongside them and then branch off to the start of the open field where more uniformed men in blue stand opposite a line of other men dressed in gray. The lines of men are mirror images. They have the same facial hair, the same sunburnt faces. I wonder which ones are the flies' fathers. They all look the same.

Fritter, meanwhile, twirls his shirt over his head. "My people!"

ONE OF THE REENACTORS LOOKS over at us, but I know he doesn't see me because I'm standing next to a nearly naked three-hundred-pound black man with a bouncing chest, his nipples like eyes all agog for the pageantry.

"Do you know what some people called the Civil War in my hometown?" Fritter says to me.

"What's that?"

"The Late, Great Unpleasantness."

"That sounds poetic."

"Yeah. Pretty fucking poetic."

We get in position next to family members who have gathered for the battle. Between the split lines of soldiers is a gulf that cuts the manicured lawn perfectly in half. The fastest way for us to reach the hospital's entrance is to just go straight across the field, right through the line of fire.

Fritter, as if reading my mind, nudges me. "You ready?"

My heart drums inside me. I suddenly want nothing more than to see my father.

The soldiers have already drawn their oiled muskets. They

are pointing them at each other. I pull away just before an officer shouts an order.

I sprint beyond being a girl in my own body.

I become an idea.

I know I'm not a woman yet.

But I'm also not a girl.

I'm a poem no one will ever translate.

I RUSH PAST THE MUSKETS as they begin spraying clouds. It's black-powder smoke that isn't smoke. They're not guns. I feel like I can look into each face I sheer past, into each eye as it aims its muzzle to put me out of my misery. I see my father, and I don't see him ever again. More clouds of smoke like nets cast in the river. Nothing touches me. Not one thread of woven smoke. You can't touch an idea. I'm too fast to catch in anyone's mind. In this moment, like Fritter, I'm invincible.

WHEN I REACH THE OTHER side of the field, I turn to face the cheering from the crowd. The roar reaches my ears. Fritter hobbles up behind me. He's clapping along with the bystanders. Some of the soldiers, Union and Confederate alike, raise themselves up from where they've fallen so they can flip me off properly. Others take out their phones to take our picture. They're capturing our image.

Amid the celebration Fritter bends over and heaves.

"We did it." I dig at a stitch in my side.

"That was all you." Fritter wipes his mouth.

The hospital's entrance is an atrium with mauve- and teal-colored couches, faux palm trees. I walk up to the front desk and ask about my father. The receptionist, an elderly white woman with a bone-colored pixie cut, clicks a few buttons on her keyboard. She says he's not here anymore.

"What does that mean?"

"It means he's gone, sweetheart."

She touches my hand. Her fingers are skinny like knitting needles, her pointy nails painted an eggshell white.

"As in *gone* gone?" I take a step back.

"I'm afraid I don't understand."

"I think what she's asking is, was he discharged?" Fritter says. "Or is he dead?"

The woman cuts her eyes at Fritter, as if only noticing him for the first time. "Sir, I'm afraid you're going to have to put on a shirt if you think you're visiting this hospital."

"Maybe I'm not visiting. Maybe I'm making my home right here."

"Then maybe I need to call security."

"If you think you need to call security, knock yourself out."

"Ma'am," I interrupt, "I'm sorry. I really need to find my father."

Fritter eyes the woman as he puts on his shirt.

The woman sighs but clicks a few buttons and then smiles, pleased with herself. She grabs the silver crucifix hanging from her necklace and slides it back and forth. "Well, what do you know? He was released not even thirty minutes ago."

"Thank you," I say.

"Yes, thank you very much," Fritter says.

"You're welcome, sweetheart." The woman studies my face now.

Fritter doesn't even blink.

The sliding doors open as a clean-shaven black man in a tailored gray suit comes through carrying balloons and a giant stuffed elephant. Bluegrass music follows in behind him. The jangle of notes makes me think of a cigar-box guitar. When the doors close, Muzak over the hospital's speakers resumes. The man looks at Fritter and nods, and Fritter nods back.

"I think I have a good idea where Dox is," Fritter says to me.

"Stop reading my mind."

Fritter raises his eyebrows and points at the receptionist. "You should hear what she's thinking. Not good. Not good at all."

"Oh, fuck off," the woman says.

WE WALK BEHIND A LINE of vendor tents. There are smoky grills that are as long as banquet tables. Aproned workers take wide paintbrushes and dunk them into buckets of brown sauce and then baste the hammered chicken breasts lined along the grates. Fritter says he could eat all of it, the entire batch and even the coals, and I nod and stop next to a white girl who looks to be my age pouring a large carton of blue liquid into a whirring machine the size of a semitruck's tire rim turned sideways.

The sides start fanning out faint strands, and the girl takes a narrow paper cone shaped like a unicorn's horn and begins to twirl it around and around, tracing the metallic circle. The strands wrap on top of each other until they bunch into a blue beehive on a stick. She holds it up and gingerly places the cotton candy into the hands of a young boy wearing a gray kepi and a neon-yellow T-shirt with a cape that's just a Confederate flag tucked into his collar.

"That's the kind of shit that scares me," Fritter whispers. "That boy right there."

"All that you've seen, and that's what scares you?"

"Hate hardwired with happiness? That's the toughest net to untangle."

Past the vendor stands is a group of musicians sitting in a circle and trading off turns, keeping a melodic riff going among them. One on a fiddle sews the melody into the scrape and strum of a mandolin player, who then hands it off to someone sliding up the neck of a cigar-box guitar.

DOX SMILES WIDE WHEN HE spots us. Those teeth of his, I swear. Most are missing, and what few remain could be stray pieces of peanut brittle. I wonder if Fritter ever worries about having his genes. Dox points to the far left with his chin, and we look over to see my father using a wooden spoon and slapping the bottom of a plastic bucket. With his vest-and-no-shirt getup, my father fits in better than any of the rest of us.

He's wrapped his hospital gown into a ball. I pretend for a moment that it's cotton candy he's bought for me, like he thinks I'm younger than I am. I feel like I've been on pause in his head for a long time, even though I've been paying attention to him, to his legs and his feet, though not as often perhaps. I could always do better.

But who has been paying attention to me?

The inside of my mouth goes slack, and I can't swallow. I'm suddenly angry with him, as if he meant to do this, as if it were solely his neglect that has brought us here. I'm not going to cry, but I'm not going to smile either.

I walk up to him and he holds out his arms. "Did you miss me?"

I can't help it. I slap him across the face.

"WHAT WAS THAT FOR?" my father says.

"Don't ever do that again."

He laughs but touches his cheek.

I slap at him, this time all over his arms. It's a storm. I keep at it until I can't see. I start crying. No one stops me. Not even Fritter. People look at us like we're not real, but I don't care.

"I hate you," I say. "I do. I hate you!"

"Honey," Dox says.

"No, let her," my father says. "Let her get it out."

My hands can only hover. I can't hit him anymore.

"It's okay, Pearl," my father says. "I was scared, too."

MY FATHER PULLS ME TO HIM and we stand there while others gather. A bearded man who isn't dressed as a reenactor but could easily be one of the regiment digs in a giant duffel bag. He pulls out spoons and rattles and all kinds of noisemakers. He turns the duffel bag over, gives it a jolt, and dumps out a few empty tin coffee cans that spin to a standstill. One lands upside down. Its dented bottom catches sunlight. That's the one I grab because I still feel like punching something. My knuckles rap the light and sound metallic. The bearded man yells, "Louder! Louder!" We keep at our banging, but now it's all in time. Dox and my father are both hopping from one foot to the other. Fritter claps, and I hoot and holler. Soon everything becomes a song.

When our revelry subsides, a few Confederate soldiers standing near a souvenir tent glance over at Fritter. They point excitedly, like they've just seen the real Stonewall Jackson. They head our way.

"You need to step your ass back," Fritter says to the first one.

"You ruined our scene," another one says, already hysterical. "We trained a long time for that battle, and you messed it up."

Other soldiers begin to walk over as well.

"What about me?" I say, stepping between them.

"What about you?" the first one says.

Fritter pats my shoulder and winks.

"They're not worth it," I say to him. "They're just flies."

"What now?" Fritter says. "Flies?"

Dox laughs. "She said they're flies."

"Fuck you," the first one says to Fritter.

"How about we go talk about this over there," Fritter says to the group of men. Dox and my father stand there like their legs have suddenly stopped working. Reenactors gather in numbers, wanting to know what's going on, wanting to see if this guy is the same asshole that ran through the field during the reenactment. Like they can't tell, like there's another Fritter in the world.

"Yeah," the first one says, "that sounds like a real good idea, boy. Let's go over and see if we can't talk about this like a bunch of civilized *folk*." The other soldiers laugh on cue, and my teeth and jaws hurt from clenching, but Fritter is all smiles, is all nods and yuck-yuck, and he even slaps one on the shoulder, like they're sharing the funniest joke they've ever heard.

The men cluster around Fritter. He has this secret he's been meaning to share with someone for a long time, and they've been chosen to hear it. It's all serious with no more jokes. When I go to follow them, my father grabs my wrist and says, "No, ma'am." I twist my arm to loosen his grip, and just as I'm about to free myself from him, Dox grabs my other wrist, and they hold me next to them.

My father says, "You don't need to see this." It's suddenly a lesson that's been scratched off the list, a translation he gave the once-over and x'ed out. He's trying to cover it up.

• • •

I follow Fritter with my eyes. I won't take my eyes off him. He looks like a torch before a procession of uniforms, blue and gray in lockstep, united, and as they pass others in the crowd, new ranks join up, and I think of White Truck and its parachute behind it. I know I was wrong. These men following behind Fritter are not flies like Main Boy and his friends. No, they're dust kicked up from a road people will always try to make use of.

The men with Fritter don't look like soldiers anymore. Most have taken off their gear. They've set their satchels on the ground next to the muskets.

"We should help him," I say.

"Wait," Dox says. "Just wait."

The circle of men turns like it's going to click into place. I move as if to take a step forward.

My father squeezes my wrist again. "Wait. Just wait."

All of the sounds of the festival can't drown out the singing I hear. For it's singing that Fritter unleashes on the soldiers. It's a singing for their hands and their knees, their foreheads even. They touch his chin. They touch his neck and his chest. He sings like he's holding the snake's mouth open and pouring the song inside it. I wait like Dox and my father told me, but I'm tired of waiting. Bodies are on him and vanish into the ground with the embers. Fritter is singing that dirge, that sweet, happy crying song he carries inside him.

The men lock arms. It's a scrum. They're all just boys playing a neighborhood game, and someone's hidden the ball inside Fritter and they're all reaching for it, trying to get at it, and I smile now because they can barely hold him down, and I think that means he's winning. Other men come to watch what's going on and figure out their role in this scene unfolding, how they're to not question what started all of this, but that they're here to answer how it will end.

How many fists clenched dreadlocks? How many were ripped clean from his head? Fritter keeps singing, and I want to yell, "I hear you!" But Dox and my father hold me back when deputies' uniforms show up and draw their glossy black wooden clubs. They want to play the game, too. They're breaking in new equipment. They want to get a chance to hit the ball as hard as they can.

I know my father would tell me not to mix metaphors, but how else to reach the confusion I harbor when the ball becomes Fritter's head and simultaneously becomes the top of a torch. Each hit sends sparks into the grass and into the trees that burst into blank, translation-less pages.

When everyone is finished, they take a step back. They're heaving, sucking wind. Fritter is on the ground. His head is patchy. There are spaces where his dreadlocks should be. I shake loose from my father and run to him. The men see me. They start walking away. I get down on the ground and cradle Fritter's head. His eyes are rolled back, but he's breathing. I hold his face in my hands.

When he comes to, he says, "How did I do?"

He wants me to smile, and I smile.

I FIND A SPIGOT AND wring out Fritter's shirt. I hand it to Dox, thinking he might want to tend to his son, but Dox shakes his head, which surprises me. I dab at places on Fritter's swollen face.

"I'm fine," Fritter says, shooing my hands away. "That was nothing."

My father says we should head home and asks where we parked the truck. I tell him how it died on the road, how we happened upon a construction site and Fritter made us a raft.

"A *raft*?" My father shakes his head.

I nod and point over at the embankment by the river. There's our contraption of a raft, splintered and all.

"You two rode that here?" Dox says.

Fritter smiles. The blood in his mouth outlines his teeth.

"A shame," my father says, "it won't be taking us back."

And just like that, our raft becomes a poem.

We walk the full length of the downtown, though it's hardly a feat. The downtown is only a handful of blocks with painted brick townhomes and storefronts sandwiching one another in a spectrum of pastels. Some of the people from the festival have been diverted to these stores like schools of fish through a series of weirs.

Crowds ripple along the sidewalks. Businesses sell antiques, mostly refurbished Civil War weapons and framed parchment papers. In little jewel boxes, pillowed in cotton, are pitted musket balls. They've been pulled from warped tree trunks or unearthed and pitched from tilled soil like random, obnoxious stones that scraped plow blades. My father wishes aloud that there could be a pawnshop close by. He points at the rusty tools in the canvas bag I'm still carrying. He thinks I don't know what he's up to, his mind already switching modes. He doesn't once ask about the rod and the creel, though I know those would be the first to go.

"If only we could get our hands on some money," he says.

A few girls my age walk by us on the sidewalk. They look back and laugh.

We pass more storefronts. In one is a pale blue summer dress. It drapes on a faceless mannequin. I turn away.

The main street ends at a cobblestone pavilion with a gazebo overlooking the bridge Fritter and I drifted under this morning. My father and Dox walk over to a bench under the gazebo and plop down. I keep forgetting my father is spent. Dox is no spring chicken either. Fritter hobbles up, takes the end next to Dox, and lets out a sigh. These men are a sad bunch.

I set our things on the ground next to Fritter.

"Where are you going?" my father says.

"Nowhere." I keep on going.

It might be good to see the dress after all.

The girls from earlier have stopped in front of the same store. They're in dresses, too, with matching suede ankle boots. Both have straight auburn hair with bangs. Their faces are drawn and long like those of baby alpacas, their eyes lashy and dark. I don't mean that as a dig. These girls are pretty in their own way.

I stop at the storefront, too, but keep my distance from them. They see me and smile.

I smile back. "Hey."

They don't answer. They laugh and walk off.

They leave me alone.

In my reflection, I see what they see. My hair is a rat's nest. My face is more dirt than face. Dried blood is on my shirt from holding Fritter's head. My chest isn't even there.

"Hey," I say to myself.

My reflection keeps laughing at me.

When I head back to the gazebo, I hear mostly minor chords and screech. My father doesn't miss a beat. He's tied the hospital gown around his neck and has a shit-eating grin on his face. With the wooden spoon, he slaps the bottom of the overturned bucket, right in the molded bull's-eye. He lifts the bucket up and down so the rim, which is flush with the ground, produces a deep-sounding bass. Fritter winces but sings. Dox is sweet Dox.

I run to them. I can't get to them fast enough.

I don't have an instrument on me, nothing to transform in the canvas bag, so I just clap quarter notes on the offbeat. I'm an echo of what my father is doing. It's not much, but it's something.

If I close my eyes, it's like we've been dropped on our pier. A part of me wants to take off my shirt and dance around to get the tourists' attention. Another part of me wants to just dance and keep clapping, so that's what I do. My chest is still flat as a block of ice. But here's the thing: I can feel that block melting.

I'm glacial and cutting through the landscape. I pull Dox,

Fritter, and my father along with me. I'm high-stepping like the red-haired woman in the framed print hanging in our old kitchen. The faces around me look painted on the air. I know this song Dox has chosen. I jump in with Fritter on the harmony of "Drown," and Dox lets out a little yell. My father keeps his head down. He tries to keep up.

People branch off from the sidewalks and come our way. Some are putting dollar bills in the basket. The dollar bills stick out the top and fill the creel like trout. Someone even places in a twenty, and when I look up to see who is being so generous, he sweeps those white bangs of his to the side and slips on his Wayfarers. He turns his back on me and walks away. The others are with him—Reese, Clint, and Everett—all except for Wythe, who stands off to the side recording us with his phone. I stop what I'm doing.

"No, keep going"—Wythe laughs—"this is pure fucking gold!"

Wythe films me, and I pretend like he's not there. It's the only way I can make it through. Main Boy and the others walk away. I follow. It's another block before Main Boy even looks back.

"Where are you going?" I say to him.

"Beat it, Pig-Pen. You're lucky I don't have you arrested."

"Me?"

"You took my dad's shit."

"Well, you deserved it."

Main Boy stops and turns around. The flies hover behind him. Wythe is still at it with the filming.

"What did you say?" Main Boy sticks his finger in my face. "Did you just fucking admit to it?"

"Yes, she did." Wythe nods at his phone.

"I didn't break anything. You can have it all back."

"I don't want it back," Main Boy says. "I wouldn't take it back anyway. Not after you've had your hands all over it."

The flies start throwing elbows.

"Burn"—Wythe laughs—"burn."

"Okay, everybody," I say. "Don't shit yourselves."

I wish the flies would wander off so I can talk to Main Boy, but there's no way they're going to miss anything. Wythe is making sure of it. He keeps holding the phone close to my face.

On the next block are the two girls with the alpaca faces. I point and Wythe sneers. He and the flies take off in their direction, leaving Main Boy and me alone.

"Did you get in trouble?" I say to Main Boy.

"Not really."

"How come?"

"Insurance. They gave him double what it was worth."

Main Boy puffs out his chest and looks around. The flies are gone.

"Wow," I say.

"I know."

"What about you? Are you angry?"

He looks at me like we've never met before, like everything has been erased and we're starting from scratch.

"I thought we had something good," he says.

I laugh.

"What? Why are you laughing?"

Fucking flies.

It's too much. It's just too much.

"What have you guys been up to?" I say. "More videos?"

"Yeah. We filmed a segment on foraging that didn't go so great. Clint ate a mushroom that almost killed him."

I try not to laugh.

"You can laugh," Main Boy says. "We all did."

"That's cold."

"I know. Then he started puking and couldn't stop. Wythe was the only one who kept laughing. Now he's on a pranking kick. Can't get enough."

"Big surprise."

"I know. I'm kind of done, actually."

"If you say so."

Main Boy glances back at the flies and then stares at the ground. "You take care of yourself, Pig-Pen."

"Yeah."

"I'm serious." He steps closer, like he's going to kiss me in broad daylight.

I take a step back. Wythe and the flies are busy chatting up the two girls. It's sad to watch, knowing what I know about those boys. I shake my head and start to walk away.

"Pearl?" Main Boy says.

I turn around. "Yeah?"

"How's Marianne Moore?"

IT'S STRANGE TO BE AROUND so many people at once. All the hubbub of the reenactment and just the town itself weighs you down. When I leave Main Boy, I have to weave my way around couples walking hand in hand. Large families are the worst. They have so many things that they own—what look like four-wheel-drive double strollers, camouflage diaper bags and matching backpacks, things that cost an arm and a leg.

Teenagers mill about a pizza shop. They've taken over the outside tables lining the sidewalk. I try not to stare at the plates of food, but the smell of the bubbling cheese is overwhelming. Through the glass windows, strings of white decorative lights hang from the ceiling. Almost all of the teenagers are wearing T-shirts that advertise for the local high school. It's where I would probably go.

Maybe one of these kids would've even been my friend.

An empty chair is at the last table. It sits off to the side, and I make a beeline for it. I want to feel what it feels like to hang out with kids my age, kids who aren't the flies, but I'm nervous. I think someone is going to grab the chair and yank it away just to get a laugh.

When I get close, I dive into the seat. It's not cool. I sit back and act normal. I take out my phone, just for something to do. I forget it was dead. It was ruined by the river anyway. No one is even looking at me. They're all talking about this party where everyone got wasted. Someone mentions the video where a kid eats a wild mushroom and then gets sick. I want to tell them I know who that kid is, I know who they're talking about. It's my chance to get in. I want to say something, at least, but I don't.

I'm right here, and it's like I'm not here at all.

I lean, trying to listen to other conversations, and the ones nearest to me get up and move closer to the group at the other tables. I'm not going to get up and move now. Someone says loudly, "God, what a dog," and the rest laugh. When I finally look over, they're all on their phones.

ON OUR WAY OUT OF TOWN, we stroll into a service station and buy bags of pork rinds and some cola for the journey. Dox says he knows the woman who owns this station. Her name is Imogene. When Imogene sees Dox, she steps out from around the counter and gives him a hug that lifts him off the ground. Maybe it's just me, but Imogene looks a lot like Fritter, like she spit him out. When I casually mention it to Fritter, he pokes my chest. "We're not all related, Pearl." I scoff, and he gets a real kick out of my reaction. He tells Dox what I said and then what Fritter himself said in response. Dox laughs and tells Imogene. Imogene laughs, and I'm horrified.

In one of the garage bays, there's a flatbed wrecker with a black Honda secured to the top. I go in to take a closer look, and my father follows. I check the front end, but there isn't even a scratch on the bumper. I breathe a sigh. My father hears me and says, "What was that for?"

"No reason. I thought I'd seen this car before, but I was wrong."

Fritter hobbles in and then it's Dox and Imogene. Dox has

his arm around Imogene's waist, and she's laughing and telling him he's as crazy as he ever was.

"This beautiful woman," Dox says, "is going to save our lives."

Dox sits in the cab of the wrecker with Imogene, who said she was hauling the car over to the next county anyway. It was no sweat off her back to drop us on the way. We put the windows down in the black Honda. Fritter gets in the passenger's seat. He scoots the seat back plenty. None of us wants to be at the wheel. I sit in the back of the car with my father. I lean against him. Our things rattle on the floorboard. From here, I can see the river on one side. Especially up high, like we are. All of it moves on its own.

"You scared me," I say.

"Him or me?" Fritter says without turning his splotchy head.

"Both of you."

Fritter laughs.

"Are you listening?" I say to my father.

"I hear you."

"You have to do better. For me."

He doesn't say anything.

"Are you listening?"

He won't answer.

That's how I know he's heard me.

WE PULL INTO THE YARD next to the broken washing machines. There's no Marianne Moore coming from around the corner, or from under the house. It tears me up inside. We try to give Imogene some of our earnings, but she won't take it.

She beeps the horn at us and is gone.

Fritter walks away, and I feel like I'm counting more patches on his head, more than what were there before.

I call for the dog.

"Probably in the woods," my father says, and goes in the house to lie down.

Dox carries his cigar-box guitar down to the pier. "C'mon, Lucille," he says, like he's B.B. King.

I take the rod, creel, and some empty cans with me, just in case the traps are full. I can hear Dox playing. The song travels downriver and follows me but keeps getting softer, like he's turning the volume down on himself.

I CALL OUT FOR MARIANNE MOORE AGAIN. She doesn't show her face. The traps are empty, so I tie on a fly. I bite off the excess line.

I try to remember what Fritter taught me. I pull out about twenty feet of line, and it immediately bunches on the water. There are branches near me, so I wade out more to get a good back cast. The current is grabby at my legs.

It's a mess at first, the bunched line, but I let the current get ahold of it and pull. The river sorts it out on its own. I didn't have to do a thing. I look over my shoulder at Dox in silhouette. He's noodling on the cigar-box guitar.

I lift the rod up slow, then fast, but it doesn't do what I want. The floating line drops like a snapped kite string. The current drags the line. I get it back in front of me. This time, I think about my mother's story.

She's on the pier again. It's evening, just like it is now. When she looks out over the river, she sees someone else. It's not Fritter as a boy. She sees me. I'm the one wading into the water and pulling back on the rod until the line forms a small loop that unrolls slowly. I'm the one writing to her on the sky.

I let the muddler sink and then start stripping the line back. The first hit comes, and when it does, I think I've snagged a branch on the bottom. It doesn't give at all. I pull up, and the line stays tight, even tightens. It zigzags for a bit, and that's when I know. Some son of a bitch is making me work for it. It's on the other end holding its ground.

Dox sees me struggling and starts playing louder. Chords slide. I'm smiling. I keep stripping in the line until the leader is the only thing left between me and this decent-size bullhead surfacing. It's a chore to free the muddler. The bullhead is all goop and river snot. God knows what else it's sucked down its gullet. I put it in the creel, cast out again, and damn if I don't hook into another one, and then another after that. The creel is overflowing. The fish start up with their grunting, making a slight ruckus. I tell them it'll all be over soon enough. The damn things get quiet like they understand me.

I slap them on the planks next to Dox. The spikes of their side fins almost pierce my hands. "Careful, now," Dox says, "let's no one get hurt." He cleans them and carries the stripped fillets inside to fry them up with cracker meal. I sit out on the pier and take it all in. I don't check on my father. I stand up and yell Marianne Moore's name once more. Nothing answers. I go inside to where it's sweltering. It's just a smidge warmer than hell.

My father is sitting in a chair while Dox cooks up the fish.

"Did you see her?" my father says to me.

"I don't know where she is."

"She'll come back. Don't worry."

"That's a switch."

"What is?"

"Sounds like you might want her back."

He doesn't bite. "She's not well, Pearl. She'll have to go at some point."

"Well, now she's gone."

"Animals do that when they're dying."

"No shit."

I SPEND DAYS GATHERING what I can: chicory root to roast for Dox's and my father's coffee, the brown cattails that taste like corn, and the small, palm-size pawpaw fruit, once they've ripened. I can smell the pawpaw from far away. Those are Fritter's favorite.

Everywhere I walk in the woods, there's a growing heat. It's the humidity, but it's also the layers of flora burning with life. Each leaf is a flame that lights up and diminishes when another takes its place. Every chance I get, I call out, "Princess! Princess!" Nothing answers to that name anymore.

I don't think about Main Boy and the flies. I expect soon there will be an eviction notice, but it's not like we own the place. I don't know what happens to people in our situation. All I know is I didn't keep up my end of the bargain with Main Boy, so maybe anything goes.

My father and Dox managed to get the truck working again. Dox takes it into town every morning to busk. My father sometimes joins him. What little money they make, they spend on a big cloth bag of rice or potatoes and the inevitable bottle of something. They share the bottle in the evenings, despite my father's knowing he shouldn't anymore. The doctor said my father needed to start taking shots for his condition. When I confront my father, he lifts the bottle and takes a long pull like I'm not even there.

"This is my prescription, right, Dox?" my father says. "How many shots does that make now?"

Fritter doesn't come out of his room.

I PASS SOME RABBIT SCAT and bend down to feel it. The scat is soft, fresh, and together, in their mound, the spheres look like tiny musket balls. Out here by myself, Fritter's voice is loudest in memory. He is guiding me through the brush. He is telling me to make a snare with some twine I weave together from nearby vines I've stripped. I pull down one of the branches, so that it bends all the way to the ground, and I tie the line and set the trap. In the middle of the loop destined for some beautiful animal's neck is pawpaw fruit I've folded open like a book.

Everywhere I look I find things that could sustain me. There are numerous edible flowers and nuts. I hear Fritter telling me to gather them all and take them back and put them in sorted piles. I strip two long branches and trim away the leaves. By hanging the cans on the opposite ends of these branches, I make a yoke for each shoulder. The deeper I walk into the woods, the heavier the load of what I've gathered becomes.

IS IT TERRIBLE TO ADMIT that when Wythe comes with the invitation, I find myself happier than I've been in a very long time? The flies haven't forgotten about me.

I emerge from the woods with all of the cans filled to the top. Hanging from my elbow like a purse is a rabbit I've snared. My father and Dox are camped out on the end of the pier. Without Marianne Moore on guard, they don't even acknowledge Wythe sitting there in his piss-yellow golf cart. Wythe is waiting for someone to take notice. When he spots me, he covers his mouth. I must amuse him to no end.

"What are you doing here?" I set down the paint cans. I hold up the rabbit.

"That's not alive. Is it?"

I cradle the animal to me. "What are you doing here, Wythe?"

"Mason wanted me to invite you to the dance."

"What dance?"

"I don't know. Something he's cooked up."

I laugh like I don't care, like my heart isn't thrashing.

"What's so funny?"

"You. The messenger."

"Okay, whatever."

"You tell Main Boy if he wants to invite me, he'll have to do it himself."

"Who the fuck is *Main Boy*?"

"I mean Mason."

Wythe laughs now. "Fucking *Main Boy*."

I don't say anything. I just pet the rabbit's head.

"Look, he feels bad, okay?"

"I really don't care."

"He could still have you all run out of here. He could put you out on your ass." Wythe snaps his fingers. "You think they'd like that?"

Wythe points at the pier.

Dox and my father are oblivious to us. Notes slide into laughter.

"I don't have anything to wear."

"He'll buy you a dress." Wythe is smiling now. "It's the least he can do, right?"

"He's not buying me a dress."

"But he will."

"I don't want him to buy me a dress. I'll get my own dress."

"So you'll go?"

I look at the river. Though it's right there in front of me, like Dox's song, I can barely make it out.

"Fine."

"Really?"

"I said fine."

"Oh, man, you're gonna make him so happy. And me, too."

"You?"

He studies the ground. "Ever since I saw you last, I've been feeling kind of bad. I shouldn't have filmed you. That was wrong. Just so you know, I didn't post any of it."

I want to say, "Congratulations, you're now a human being." But that might be pushing it.

Before Wythe climbs back in his golf cart, he tells me the details. The dance isn't at the school but at a warehouse the rising seniors all chipped in to rent so they can drink there and not get caught. Mason can't pick me up beforehand because he's still waiting on a new golf cart.

"Is that cool to just show up?" Wythe says.

"That's cool."

Before Wythe pulls away, I stop him.

"What is it?"

I don't care how I sound. "Why me?"

He doesn't even hesitate. "Because he wants to show you off, Pearl."

I TELL MY FATHER ABOUT the dance, and he says absolutely not. I try to tell him who Mason Boyd is, that his father bought up all of the land nearby, and my father smirks, like I don't know what I'm talking about.

"I already told you we're not squatters."

I want to believe it, to believe how my father thinks all of this around us, even if we could buy it and put our name on the deed, would still be borrowed: the land, the money it represents, the river that doesn't care whether we're here to drift on it or not. All of it is borrowed, he would say.

I shrug and leave it alone. I can't bring myself to believe any of his shit right now. All I know is there's this dance that will happen whether my father wants it to or not.

"This is the same boy?" my father says.

"What do you mean the *same* boy?"

"The one you were running with."

"I wasn't running with anyone."

"Pearl."

"I wasn't."

"Okay. Is it the boy you would visit on occasion? Is that better, more precise for you?"

"We didn't visit."

"Now you're being obtuse."

"I'm sorry I'm being obtuse."

"Whatever it is you did together."

"We didn't do anything."

"Is it the same one? Is it the same boy?"

"I just want to go to the dance."

"Since when do you care about dances?"

"I've always cared about them."

"I'm just trying to understand you."

"You're just trying to understand me?"

"Let's start over."

"Okay, let's."

"I don't want you to go," he says.

I hear Dox playing a riff outside. It's not a happy song. "Why?"

"Because you're my daughter, and I don't know anything about this boy or who will be there." My father crosses his arms and I get a glimpse of his former self, but he and I both know he's so far past that, it won't hold. "You know, you're asking a lot of me."

I bite my tongue.

"You are. When you're a parent, you'll understand."

"I will never be a parent. I wouldn't dare bring a child into this world."

My father does a slow blink.

"Sorry, but I wouldn't."

"You keep running with this boy, and—"

"And what?"

"Don't make me say it."

"You think I don't know how it works."

"I'm sure you know."

"I haven't even started."

"What are you talking about?"

"*Started?* I'm not repeating myself, not to my father."

He forces a cough. "Well, that doesn't matter. You know you can tell me these things."

"It's not fair. I shouldn't have to tell you these things."

"I know."

"I'm talking about something else."

"I know. I'm sorry."

MY FATHER GOES BACK TO his typewriter and his pages. It's all sadness, and I can't stand it. Dox, on the other hand, gathers all of Fritter's old T-shirts for me, and even some of the curtains. We just need materials.

Though we have a yard full of washing machines, the irony is that we don't have electricity to run even one of them. I take the bundle and scrub them by the river. I don't even keep an eye out for moccasins and copperheads anymore. I wash the shirts and curtains and wring the river out of them and hang them on branches.

After they've dried, Dox tells me he could soak them in a pan of transmission fluid, to give them a little color.

"Maybe next time," I say.

He points at me and laughs.

We rinse the shirts and curtains again, and Dox fills empty cans with sassafras and other aromatic herbs. We let them soak and dry again. Gone is Fritter, all the ripeness of him. Dox takes my measurements. I blush when he wraps the measuring tape around my waist and then around my bust.

"Can you give me some boobs?"

"I was thinking something simple."

"Elegant."

"Yes. Elegant."

He salvages large cuts of cloth and fashions them into wide panels that he stretches across the floor in his room. With tailor's chalk, he marks dotted lines along the edges. He lets me watch him work. The light blue marks make me think of the map Main Boy has of the county, how each line is a demarcation of property.

"So what can you tell me about him?" Dox says. "What's this boy like?"

"You've seen him."

"When?"

"When we were playing. He's the guy who put a twenty in the basket."

"Oh, yeah. Mr. Big Bucks. Mr. Sunglasses."

"His family is rich."

"Like I said. Mr. Big Bucks."

"You also said he looked like Andy Warhol."

"I did?"

"Yeah."

"Does that boy wear a wig, too?"

"No, it's his real hair."

"And how would you know?"

"I touched it, Dox. It's real."

"Uh-huh."

THE MORNING OF THE DANCE, I wake before the others. The sun hasn't come up yet. I still look in the corners of rooms. I want to see Marianne Moore step out of the shadows. I run my hand along the dress.

"Sweet Dox," I whisper, and keep moving.

When I pass Fritter's room, I expect to see him sprawled on his mattress or turned onto his side with those pink splotches of scar tissue I'd seen during our float on the river. All I see, instead, are the painted walls. It's all black, from the floor to the ceiling. I wonder if this means he's finished.

In the kitchen, I take the cluster of old soap bars we've squeezed together. I cut off a slice like it's a sliver of cake. In the corner are the fly rod and the creel that don't belong to me.

Trees begin to fill with sunlight. I shake my head. They're just trees. I push away branches with my free hand. The branches swing back and cover the path behind me. I can smell myself. I smell like my father. I smell like Dox when he opens his mouth. I smell like Marianne Moore's matted fur that would sit in clumps on her back.

Yet there's one thing I'm certain of, and it's that I don't smell like my mother. It's something else I've forgotten. It's like she never existed.

I take off my clothes and leave them on the bank. I hold the soap to my nose and take a deep breath. I drop the soap with my clothes and pick up the rod and the creel and wade into the water. I'm careful where I step. There are a few large rocks, but it's mostly a muddy bottom. My reflection isn't me.

My face isn't even mine.

What does Main Boy even see in me?

But I can't help smiling. I think about the dress Dox made. I smile when I picture myself in that dress and Main Boy watching me walk into the room. All eyes will be on me for a change, and not in a bad way.

I fish the floating line through the guides of the rod and tie on to the end of the leader the same muddler I'd used to catch the bullheads the other day. I get some excess line in front of me. I false cast. I pull back and go forward, feeling the rod tip load and unload. Once I've found my rhythm, I open my eyes to see the line hovering. I'm naked in the water. *Don't even think about it.*

The floating line goes back and forth.

It leaves me and returns to me.

There is no translation for the ache I feel.

I get skunked by the river. Nothing rises. Nothing hits. I return the rod and the creel to the bank, and I grab the soap. It's going to dry out my hair, but I don't care. Better that than have it reek. I lather my entire body. My eyes burn.

The river slips over me and I hold my breath. It's warmer in the shallows. I crouch down, pressing my feet into the muddy bottom. I push off like I'm my father launching off the end of the pier.

The deeper into the river I go, the cooler the water becomes. I sink into it, and the river wraps around me. When I surface, I see a few sailboats in the distance. They're tiny. Their open sails are like the petals of fragrant water lilies. My father would say *Nymphaea odorata*.

I step out of the water, but I don't dry off. I don't want to use my old clothes. This is my body. Even if I had a clean towel, something from Main Boy's bathroom closet that was fluffy and perfectly folded, I wouldn't use it. I gather up everything and carry it through the woods. The air warms even more.

I try to keep the leaves from brushing my arms. I don't care how stupid I sound, I go in search of a corsage. There are so many things flowering. A bunch of spatterdock and pickerel-weed. There's too much to choose. I walk until my hair dries by itself.

Instead of heading toward the field where I first met Main Boy, I go off in the opposite direction. I keep west until the path vanishes and the rest of the woods pull away easily. What are left are small marsh islands thick with corollas of spartina and cattails. I don't walk out to them. The sailboats from earlier look larger, though they're still a ways away.

When I get back to the boathouse, I find the truck gone. I call out for my father, but no one answers. I peek inside the kitchen and say Dox's name, but again, it's only silence. I run inside and find some clean underwear, and I slip on the dress, too. Dox made it long, so that it sweeps along the floor.

"This way," he said, when we were doing the fitting, "they can't see you wearing those trifling shoes."

"What's wrong with these shoes?" I laughed.

I knew they were barely shoes.

"Mercy me, mercy me." Dox shook his head. "If I were you, I'd just go barefoot."

Dox told me he first met her when he used to work for her uncle. Dox had even helped him build this boathouse, but then Dox went off, left his family, and lived in a bunch of places. He worked all kinds of jobs, from construction to apprenticing with a tailor, and when Dox came back through town, the uncle had been sick for a long time and needed someone to run his boats. Most of the boats were sold off to pay the mortgage on the land.

Dox stayed on and worked the river, mainly because the uncle's wife was still living in town, and according to Dox, she was always good to him, giving him a place to live, even the run of the boathouse if he wanted. By this time, my mother had stopped coming to visit. Dox said he always wondered what had become of her.

In his mind, she still had that girl body from all those summers before, all tan and gangly. She loved to jump off the pier. He remembered her as being fearless. This was a trait I could never assign to my father.

"I worry my father and I are the same person."

"Maybe you are, but you're her, too. I can see it plain as day."

I didn't tell him that's what I was afraid of.

THEY FIND ME IN THE kitchen boiling rice for a late breakfast. I'm wearing the dress, and it's so humid, my hair sticks against the sides of my face. I ask Dox to help me braid it later.

Fritter comes through the door. His head is shorn down to skin. I almost don't recognize him. There are scars on top of his head. He touches them lightly when he sees me noticing.

"What happened to your hair?" I say.

"Got it cut."

"Makes it look like you're in the army."

Fritter won't meet my eyes now.

EVENING COMES. I WALK OUT to the pier to see my father, Dox, and Fritter. The men are sitting at the end. My father is quiet as Dox worries over the fretboard.

"I'm going," I say.

"Then go already." My father laughs for no good reason.

I wait until he has his moment. I say it again but he only shakes his head.

"Well, what do you think?" I hold out my arms. I twirl in place.

My father looks at Dox and asks if he has any dollar bills left.

"You don't have to be mean," I say.

"Then go, so you don't have to listen to me being mean."

Fritter says he wants to be the one to drive me to the dance.

My father is wearing his pin-striped vest with no shirt. The top button droops. One good pull and it will break. Next to him is the bottle they've all been sharing. I've stopped asking him what the doctor said. I walk over and kick the bottle into the river. It bobs. Without hesitating, my father goes in after it, like he's saving a child.

. . .

It's Dox who puts down his guitar and comes up to me. He touches the sides of my hair, which he helped me braid and sweep back. He kisses my forehead. I think he might say some words for us all. I'm hoping he will. Instead, he returns to his seat and slips his pale feet back in the water. The guitar lies upside down. It looks like an oar. Dox's body heaves, but there's no sound. My father lifts the bottle onto the pier and climbs up the side ladder.

"Wash your face off," my father says.

"You know I'm not wearing any makeup."

"It looks like you are."

"Thank you."

"I didn't mean that in a good way."

"Yes, you did."

Dox grins wide and his lips split. I see the gaps in his side teeth.

"I just don't want you to get hurt," my father says.

I shake my head now.

"What's so funny?" he says.

"You."

"I'm serious."

"I know. I am, too."

FRITTER HOLDS OPEN THE DOOR for me. His head is so shiny. I wipe my face with my arm. The ride to the main road takes nothing. We pass the empty field. Down the road, I see where kudzu drapes. Everything is tangled.

"We could just keep going," Fritter says.

"Sure thing. Let's go and find our raft."

"Don't tempt me. I'll do it."

Because it's starting to get dark, I focus my attention on the engine and the rattles in the fenders that come from the bumps in the road. Some lights shoot across my eyelids, but I don't budge. I stay that way until we eventually slow. When I open my eyes, I see stoplights. Increments of red mark the town. At the far end, buildings scatter and eventually dissipate back into fields.

When our stoplight turns green, Fritter stares at me. Cars gathered behind us begin to honk. The air fills with their frustration. People on the sidewalk stop what they're doing and glance over at us. All the stoplights up ahead have finally turned green, but all we can do is sit there. We try our hardest not to bust out laughing.

. . .

We pull into the parking lot. We drive over to the side and find a row of golf carts. Fritter asks me to check the directions again, that maybe we're in the wrong place.

"These boys must be assholes," Fritter says.

"They're all right. They're just boys."

"You want me to go in with you?"

"Yeah, that wouldn't be weird at all."

The parking lot is a powder of crushed oyster shells. I sink into every step. I lift the bottom of my dress so it doesn't get covered in the dust. When I get to the door, I turn and Fritter is still there in the pickup. The vehicle looks abandoned. The inside of it is empty of any light.

I PULL ON THE HANDLE and the door into the building opens easily. An overhead bulb makes the wide hallway glow yellow. I can see I'm leaving my footprints on the floor. At the end is a set of swinging doors with blackened-out windows.

"Hello?"

The floor is slick and cold. It's like I'm walking on fish. I push through the swinging doors. The room ahead is dark, save for a single chair at the opposite end that sits directly under a light stand with mounted lamps.

Beyond it is another door. I call out again. The space is cavernous and swallows my voice. I think I hear people in the shadows. I smooth my dress. The way Dox was able to bunch the top of it makes it look like something is there.

"Mason?"

There's no answer.

I look down at the floor. The floor is no longer cold. My legs are suddenly burning. There's no one here. It's all a setup, just another joke. A part of me wants to run, but I don't. The warmth rises into my chest and up into my throat. I won't scream. I won't give them the satisfaction. I don't care how stupid I look standing here.

• • •

Just for a moment, I pretend that there is music, and the flies are dressed in black suits, and there are other girls here who are my age, maybe even the alpacas but who aren't bitches and who will see me and not scoff at what I'm wearing and not tell others that I'm a slut, and not snub me in the bathroom when I go there to check my face. I study my wrist and see the ghost of the corsage Main Boy would have bought for me. It is so light and delicate it has no choice but to evaporate when someone comes up behind me and throws a hood over my head.

"WHAT THE FUCK is she wearing?"

"It's a dress, dumbass."

Someone wraps rope around my chest.

"Why would she wear a dress to this?"

"Because she's a girl."

"That doesn't make sense. Why didn't she wear the jumpsuit?"

"I didn't give her the jumpsuit."

"Why didn't you give her the jumpsuit?"

"Shut the fuck up. She's here, isn't she?"

Someone loosens the rope and tells me they're only doing it so I can change into clothes they keep pushing against me. I go to pull off the hood, and someone grabs my wrist.

"I don't think so," they say.

"What does she think she's doing?"

"I don't know. I don't care."

"She needs to change."

Someone laughs.

"I'll change her," another voice says.

More laughter.

. . .

I try to look through the hole in the hood, but I can't see anyone's face. The hood smells like Italian dressing, like they've been sitting around eating catered food all day and using this one hood as a napkin.

"Peekaboo," someone says. "I see you."

"She's trying to look."

"Fuck her. Let her look."

My hands are free now, but I don't try to take off the hood. Instead, I try to take off the dress Dox made for me, and someone says, "You're taking too long," and rips the straps and it falls into a bunch by my ankles.

"Why did you do that, dumbass?"

"She was lollygagging."

"He said gagging," someone else says.

More laughter.

"Look, she's not wearing a bra."

"So, she doesn't even have tits."

"Mason said she was a good fuck, though."

"Yeah, but I like there to be tits."

"Listen to you."

"Whoa, that's a bush."

"That's a fucking jungle."

"Why isn't she wearing underwear?"

"Because she's wild."

"I told you. Didn't I tell you?"

"That's the biggest bush I've ever seen."

"It's not a bush. It's a whisker biscuit."

"Biscuits and gravy."

More laughter.

. . .

I feel my way into the jumpsuit and zip it shut.

"Where are your shoes?" someone says.

I don't answer.

"She needs shoes. Did anyone bring shoes?"

"Fuck the shoes. The jumpsuit is enough."

Someone walks me over and makes me take a seat in the chair. It's warm from the lights shining down on it. They tie my arms behind my back and cinch the rope around my waist and then to the bottom legs of the chair. They wrap my ankles as well.

"Who has the camera?"

"Me."

"Turn it on, dumbass."

"It's on."

"Keep it on."

"It's on."

When they pull off the hood, I count four of them. They're dressed alike, in all black, with black ski masks over their faces. They're the same stupid person, except one of them is holding a knife. Its blade is white. There's a tripod with a camera on top. They've been filming this.

"Aren't you going to scream?" one of them says.

I don't say anything.

"She has to scream," another says. "Otherwise, it won't look realistic."

"You want it to look realistic? I can make it realistic."

"Who brought the blood?"

"She did."

More laughter, all eyes crinkling.

· · ·

"You want it realistic?" the one holding the knife says, but he's not talking to me. He's talking to the others. I stare at the camera and don't open my mouth. He stands beside me and makes the pose. My eyes glaze over.

"Look," he says to the others, "we have an opportunity here."

"Go on."

"I think we started this scene too soon. We should start over. Where's her dress?"

Someone walks over and grabs the dress.

"This is a fucking rag."

"Are you on the rag?" someone asks me.

"Ask her again."

"Are you on the rag?"

I don't say anything.

"Let's get a video of her changing back into the dress."

They all look at me.

"You can do that, right?"

I realize they're talking to me.

I don't say anything.

"Mason said she's wild."

"She looks wild."

"She looks like a fucking dog, but okay."

"A bitch in heat."

"Yeah, fucking bitch in heat."

"Are we doing our original idea or not?"

"She doesn't look surprised now."

"We can splice it together. I have a shot of her face seeing the knife."

"Are you scared?" they ask me.

I don't say anything.

"She's a fucking bitch."

"Yeah."

"Yeah."

The one holding the knife puts the blade up to my throat.

"God, I could just do it right now. It would be so easy to take her head off."

"We need a green screen."

"Fuck the green screen."

The one with the knife puts it to my neck and presses.

"Get her down on her knees. She needs to be on her knees."

"I think you're hurting her," *someone says.*

"Am I hurting you?" *the one with the knife says.*

I don't say anything.

I know it's Wythe. He's trying to sound like Main Boy.

"See?" *he says.* "I'm not hurting her, dumbass."

I feel dizzy. All of the lights go dim at the same time. It's as if someone put the hood back on my head, but that's not it. The room is painted black. There are no more lights. I hear the boys scream, and I hear someone saying, "Don't even think about it," *and I hear what sounds like things tearing and breaking apart, like fire crackling from branches being thrown into the blaze. I try my hardest to look into the darkness, but I can't make out all of the shapes colliding into one another. I just know when the lights come back on, I see Fritter standing in front of me.*

"Are you okay?" *he says.*

"I'M OKAY."

There are no more flies, except for Wythe, who's off to the side. His mask has been ripped off his head, but he's still holding the knife, waving it around like a TV remote.

"Get your punk ass over here," Fritter says to him.

"Fuck you, man."

Fritter laughs. "Give me the knife, boy."

"Fuck off, coon!"

Fritter grimaces. "Give me the knife and maybe I'll let you walk out of here with that little dick between your legs."

Wythe makes as if to place the knife on the floor and but then charges Fritter. Fritter grabs Wythe's wrist and tries to bend it, but the knife goes into Fritter's side. Fritter pulls it out. The knife falls to the floor. If it made a sound, I couldn't tell you what it was.

Fritter keeps bending Wythe's wrist.

"You're hurting me," Wythe says, dropping to his knees.

"Get the knife," Fritter says to me.

I grab it off the floor and walk over to Fritter. I hand it to him.

"No, I don't want it." He bends back Wythe's arms, wrapping both wrists with rope.

"I don't want it either," I say.

"Yes, you do."

"Pearl, this isn't funny," Wythe says. "We were just kidding. We were going to let you go."

"He thinks he's apologizing," Fritter says, like Wythe isn't here.

"We were going to let you go. You have to believe me, Pearl. We were going to let you go."

"You think that's the truth?" Fritter touches the wound. "Do you think he was going to let you go? He was never going to let you go."

I grip the knife. The world rushes inside my body.

"Do it," Fritter whispers. "He's a punk ass. We'll put all of his pieces in the river. They'll never find him. You know they'll never find him."

"No!" Wythe starts crying. "You have to believe me, Pearl."

I want to believe him, but I know he wasn't going to let me go.

I glance at Wythe, but I don't see him.

My head is ringing, "Princess! Princess!"

THERE IS NOTHING I WANT more than to cut away the truth, and I know where it is now. It's made a little home inside Wythe's neck. Just like the growth made a home inside my mother's chest and then hid in her brain and in other parts of her body. She became someone else entirely.

Now that I see it so clearly before me, now that I have this one chance, I'm going to take the knife and cut it away. I'm going to open it up like I'm picking the lock on a door, like there's a girl and her mother on the other side of the door, inside the boy's neck. I need to get to the mother before it's too late. Before her mother drifts away and never comes back.

The worst thing I've ever seen is my mother smiling. For just a moment, she wanted me to put the pills in my mouth. She was supposed to take me with her. Sometimes I wish I could have gone.

I go to thrust the knife into Wythe's neck, but Fritter stops me short.

I can smell Wythe now. He's pissed himself. He's crying louder.

"I knew you could do it," Fritter says to me. "I knew you could."

Wythe opens his eyes. He laughs and cries at the same time.

I'm angry at first, until Fritter starts singing.

The flies are all gone now, even Wythe. They took their golf carts and drove away, but they left behind Mason's camera and light stand. Fritter goes scavenging while I change back into my dress. I tie knots in the straps to keep the dress from falling down. I wonder if Dox will be able to salvage it or just change it into something else entirely.

We load the camera and the light stand into the back of the pickup, along with a box of paint and an array of brushes Fritter scores from one of the storage rooms. On the ride back, he asks me if I erased the footage on the camera, and I say I did, but I didn't.

When we get home, I can hear Dox and my father on the pier. Fritter has stopped bleeding, but he needs stitches. He walks out there. It's like nothing has changed.

When Dox sees Fritter, he freezes.

"How the hell did this happen?" my father says.

"I was playing with a knife," Fritter says, and looks at me. "It was my own damn fault."

"Is that true, Pearl?" my father says.

I run in the house and bring out needle and thread. Dox is already washing the wound with the little from what's left in the bottle. Fritter doesn't even wince. He just looks at his father the entire time. Even when Dox begins to close him back up. Fritter stares, and Dox weeps.

IN THE MORNING, DOX GLANCES up from a book he's reading. He sips his coffee and says, "It's instant, if you want some." I shake my head, and he studies me.

I shrug.

"That's it?" he says. "That's all I get?"

I smile, but it's not enough. Dox waits for me to keep going.

Fritter limps past us with the new cans of paint. I want him to summarize the night, but he's already closed his door behind him. Dox keeps waiting. I don't say anything.

"Oh, you should've seen it," Dox says. "There were all these girls there, but my dress was the best. And Andy Warhol was there, and he couldn't take his eyes off of me. Everyone had their eyes on me."

Dox takes a sip of his coffee and grins.

"What did Fritter say about it?" I say.

"Nothing."

"He's not talking?"

"Not a word."

FOR THE NEXT WEEK, it's a feast of quiet. My father keeps the door shut. I check the traps, but nothing gets stuck. The river keeps doing its thing. The fish that live within it pay no attention to the flies I cast. I walk the woods and call for Marianne Moore, but she doesn't answer. She's gone. She was the smartest of all of us.

I expect the sheriff to come out here at any moment, whether to arrest Fritter for what he did or to hammer up a NO TRESPASSING sign. When I come back from my walks, there's Dox on the back porch drinking another cup of instant coffee. That's it. He's tired of the chicory, I suppose.

In the evening, the window is a speaker for the song coming from the pier. Dox slides the notes, and my father punctuates them on the refrain. I wait for Fritter to blast the chorus, but he's stopped singing. The rest of the song stops as well. I hear a splash. I poke my head out the window. I can only see Dox glowing there in the darkness. I can't see my father and I can't see Fritter.

"Come here, Pearl," my father's voice says, but it could be the river talking.

I rush down the stairs. Dox is alone.

"Where are they?"

He points down at the water.

I can't see anything. They've both gone under. When they surface, they're each holding an end. I don't want it to be true, but it's true.

"It's still alive?" I say.

My father looks up from the river. He is smiling. "Did you miss me?" he says, moving the fish's mouth.

Dox says we shouldn't eat it because who knows what diseases have bored into the meat. Fritter says we can't eat it because it fought and deserves respect, that it's the second-toughest fucking thing he's ever seen. He winks at me.

The blue cat is still as big as it is in my memory. Even though they're pretending like it's alive, I know it's not. Everything has been feeding on it. It's been at the mercy of the river for a long time.

"I'm sorry," I say to my father.

"Why are you sorry?" he says.

I reach down and place my hand on the fish, but it doesn't move at all.

Fritter cradles the blue cat to him and floats on his back. He is singing, but it's not singing. It's something else I can't quite name. I just feel it. It takes being alive to sing the way he does. He is guiding the thing back to where it came from. He is going home into the darkness, and he will make it back. He has already shown me it can be done.

THE NEXT MORNING, MY FATHER says it's about time we pawned the camera and the lights we brought back, and while we're at it, the rod and creel, too. I ask him how he knows about the camera, and he says nothing ever gets by him. He wants it all gone. He thinks we'll get so much money that we can take a vacation. I tell him I thought we were already on vacation. Dox hears this part and laughs.

The traps are full, but I haven't brought any empty cans to carry the crayfish back. I drop the canisters of chicken wire and they bubble as they descend back into the river. I take the path and find the long net reset. The posts twitch. I wade out and find it's a bunch of pumpkinseeds that are tangled up. They are bright-striped aqua and yellow faces with black dots tattooed behind their gills. I unwrap the lines of monofilament from their bodies, and they dart away like I'm flinging cards across a room.

"You're welcome," I say.

When I get back to my room, the camera and the lights are gone. A horn is honking. I stare out over the yard filled with washing machines. My father is sitting behind the wheel of the pickup. A tarp is in the back. He waves me down.

I climb in the cab. "Where's my stuff?"

"*Your* stuff. Listen to you."

"It is my stuff."

"You took it, Pearl."

"So what?"

"So, it's not yours."

"It's not yours either."

"That's right, it's not mine. But it'll get us some money."

"We don't need money."

We both laugh.

I study the side of the boathouse. He follows my eyes.

"That's something else we'll need to fix," he says.

We're going to give it all back. This was his plan all along. We pass the speed-limit signs that are blown off their posts. The ones still standing are riddled with buckshot. The river is so faithful. It runs alongside us. The water looks clear to me now, but I know it's an illusion. It's there when it's not there, no matter whether I can envision it or not.

"Turn here," I say.

"Here?"

"Yeah, where the fountain is."

"The marble seems a bit unnecessary."

"I think it's all supposed to be an oasis."

"An oasis from what?"

We make the turn into Main Boy's neighborhood and follow around the traffic circle. Our pickup rattles. We have to slow to let a number of bloated men in golf carts zip across the road to reach the green on the other side. I keep watching my father's face. We pass house after house, each one a larger river-rock-and-cedar-shake monstrosity than the last.

My father says, "You know, I could've been a golfer. Dox sometimes talks about the game. He used to work at a golf course. Did you know that?"

"Not here?"

"God no." My father grins. "No, when he was younger. Back when he was with Fritter's mother."

"But Dox didn't stay to raise him."

"He came back."

"Like that means something."

"It does in my book."

We pass more houses.

People are living their lives.

"Would you ever want to play golf?" he says.

My father slows to let more golf carts cross.

"It seems kind of stupid."

He smirks. "Why stupid?"

"I see people doing it, but I don't think they're happy doing it."

"I'm sure they are, Pearl."

"I mean, I think it's an act."

I know he wants me to keep going.

"They get all dressed up just to drive around in carts and get drunk."

"Sounds pretty good to me."

I don't take the bait.

"But to play the game, you try to make as few mistakes as possible?"

"Sure."

"You have to be precise."

"That sounds about right."

He laughs.

"So what if you're a *fatalist* at heart?" I say.

We park in front of Main Boy's house.

"This is absurd," my father says. "How many kids do they have in there?"

"Just one."

I get out, prepared to confront Main Boy, but there's nothing I want to say to him. I've erased the footage. Some of it is probably still out there, but I don't care. Whatever it was we did together is all in the past anyway. I only wish I could say no one got hurt. I grab the things out of the truck and set them in a pile on the porch. The fly rod goes on last. I even go so far as to ring the doorbell, but I don't wait for anyone to answer.

Dox and Fritter have started on the construction. There's plenty of plywood, but I can see we're going to need two-by-fours and lots of them. Fritter asks me if I think our raft is still at the park by the bridge, that maybe we can break it apart and bring some of the wood back in the pickup. I say, "Don't even think about it," and Dox gets a kick out of that. He doesn't have to say what we all know, what we all believe. We'll get it from somewhere, even if it's somewhere else. We'll find a way.

I go in our house, and when I pass Fritter's door, I can see his new work. All of the walls are a silvered blue that blends into lavender at the very top. On the floor are the open cans of paint he had taken from the warehouse. There are trays with used roller brushes steeped in what's left over. I step inside the room.

The old mural is gone. Everything has been painted to look bright, like the side of a giant shad. I feel like I'm standing in the middle of the ocean, or I've just come from there, my anadromous body on the long journey upriver to spawn, my mind so clear with purpose.

I take out my journal and start writing. I remember something my mother once told me: "Don't be afraid, Pearl, or you'll just be like everyone else." I wish I could have summoned these words sooner. But I'm not sure I would have made it here, thinking of myself as a girl with the whole world still in front of her.

HELLO, MY NAME IS *Marianne Moore. I don't know how it was possible, but I could suddenly see everything. It was like I was in the sky floating above them all. I watched as they piled the scrap wood left over from fixing the side of the boathouse. It was a considerable pile. I could see the girl and hear her thinking about the river and how her father finally told her the truth about the property. All of it had been sold, except for where they were. Her mother had put what was left of the land in the girl's name. Now the girl was the beneficiary of a dream.*

The girl's father meets them out in the field. He is carrying a milk crate filled with the typed onionskin pages of the woman's unfinished manuscript, all the notebooks held together with a belt. He pulls at the typed pages like they're petals. He feeds the petals into the fire. Inside the notebooks is the woman's cursive writing, the ongoing record of her trying to find the right word, to get as close to the original meaning as possible. In the end, she ran out of ways to express herself, and that's the brutal, beautiful truth.

· · ·

The girl's father undoes the belt and tightens it around his waist. His pants are bigger on him now that he doesn't drink anymore. Dox says he'll wait to see if the girl's father's promise holds before he'll take the pants in for him. The sky gets darker now. The girl tends to the fire while Dox plays his cigar-box guitar. Fritter is singing louder than I've ever heard him sing, and the girl's father is clapping his hands and trying to keep up. The fire is so bright. I close my eyes. There's no other way to describe it. It grows brighter.

ACKNOWLEDGMENTS

I'm grateful to everyone at FSG for supporting this work. I wish nothing short of a lifetime of rivers filled with native fish for my brilliant and killer editor, Emily Bell. Her guidance throughout the writing and shaping of this book has been unparalleled. Tight lines, too, for Jonathan Galassi, Jackson Howard, Na Kim, Sean McDonald, Devon Mazzone, Steven Pfau, Jeff Seroy, and the rest of the wonderful team working behind the scenes to give Pearl a life. I'm indebted to you all.

Scott Brotemarkle and Luke Johnson were with me for the first shad run. Out of those early mornings of standing waist-deep in a frigid river, Fritter's joy materialized.

I also found inspiration from the following artists, family, friends, and places: my brothers and sisters, my mother and father, James Baldwin, Melissa Bashor, Khris Baxter, Blind Pilot, Eric Bonds, David Bowie, Maurice Browne, Rob Butler, Laura Bylenok, Peter Chang's, Jen Chang, Cathy Linh Che, Ken Chen, Yvon Chouinard, Alicia Christensen, Ralph Cohen, Harry Crews, Chris Dombrowski, Greg Donovan, Marguerite Duras, Claudia Emerson, The Faction, Tarfia Faizullah, Gisele Firmino, Brian Flanary, Fleet Foxes, Mary Flinn, Chris Foss, Kevin Goldberg,

Myla Goldberg, Rigoberto González, Jim Harrison, Jonathan Haupt, Cathy Park Hong, Cindy Horne and Barb Toellner, Hurray for the Riff Raff, Hyperion Espresso, Kent Ippolito, Chris Irvin, Marcus Jackson, Jeff Jones, Allison Joseph, Richard Katrovas, Mary Kayler, Sally Keith, my *Kundiman* barkada, Laurie Kutchins, Chris Lessick, Ada Limón, Rebecca Lindenberg, Wayne Martin, Adrian Matejka, Marie McAllister, Dave McCormack, Jim McKean, The Milk Carton Kids, Thorpe Moeckel, Nick Montemarano, John Moore, The National, Neutral Milk Hotel, Aimee Nezhukumatathil, Jessy Ohl, Orvis Woodbridge, Richard Owen, Alan Michael Parker, Persea Books, Pixies, Robert Polito, Josh Poteat, Colin Rafferty, Ladette Randolph, Ron Rash, Gary Richards, River Rock Outfitter, Warren Rochelle, Kristen Elias Rowley, Mara Scanlon, Phyllis Schirle, Dave Selover, John Shepherd, Daniel Slager, Charles Small, Son Volt, Rhonda and Matt Starcher, Phil Tabakow, Bill Tester, Jon Tribble, Trout Unlimited, Dan Tucker, R. A. Villanueva, David Wojahn, and my amazing colleagues and students in the MFA program at Queens University of Charlotte and at the University of Mary Washington.

An extra round of bear hugs for Oliver de la Paz, Fred Leebron, Sarah Gambito, Joseph Legaspi, Patrick Rosal, and Tim Seibles.

I have it on good authority that Pearl's mother spent time with Graham Robb's exquisite biography *Rimbaud* and with the work of Paul Valéry.

Lastly, this book simply would not exist without the love of Amy, Emma, and Luke. They are my fire.

A NOTE ABOUT THE AUTHOR

Jon Pineda is a poet, memoirist, and novelist living in Virginia. His memoir, *Sleep in Me*, was a 2010 Barnes & Noble Discover Great New Writers selection, and his novel *Apology* was the winner of the 2013 Milkweed National Fiction Prize. His recent poetry collection, *Little Anodynes*, won the 2016 Library of Virginia Literary Award. He teaches in the MFA program at Queens University of Charlotte and at the University of Mary Washington.